The BOOB GIRLS III

The Burned Out Old Broads at Table 12

Sandhills and Shadows

A Novel by Joy Johnson

Cover design by Janet Sieff, Centering Corporation

Copyright 2011 Joy Johnson
ISBN: 978-1-56123-231-4

Library of Congress information on file.

GRIEF ILLUSTRATED PRESS

PO Box 4600
Omaha, NE 68104

Order from: www.centering.org
1-866-218-0101 or 1-402-553-1200
centeringcorp@aol.com
www.theboobgirls.com

The BOOB Girls III: the Burned Out Old
Broads At Table 12
In *Sandhills and Shadows*

A Novel by Joy Johnson

Copyright 2011
Joy Johnson

ISBN:1-56123-231-9
Library of Congress information on file

Grief Illustrated Press
Order from: Centering Corporation
www.centering.org
1-866-218-0101 or 402-553-1200

BOOB Girl cover designs by
Janet Sieff,
Executive Director Centering Cooperation

If you enjoy this book, you'll want to go with the BOOB Girls on their earlier adventures.

The BOOB Girls:
The Burned Out Old Broads at Table 12.

The BOOB Girls II:
The Burned Out Old Broads at Table 12
in Lies, Spies and Cinnamon Rolls

Visit the girls and Joy Johnson at
www.theboobgirls.com

- Form your own BOOB Girls Group
- Blog with joy and each of the girls
- www.welcometotheboobgirls.blogspot.com
- Share your own BOOB Girl moment

Visit Joy Johnson on Facebook

Dedicated to all my BOOB Girl buddies.

You know who you are.

Wiley, dressed in his usual business suit, neatly groomed and looking judgmental with his arms folded across his chest. They were staring unashamedly at the four women sitting at Table 12 near the big floor-to-ceiling windows of the dining room.

Mary Rose McGill had both hands out, palms turned up. Next to her, leaning forward in her chair was a beautiful gypsy. She was holding Mary Rose's right hand and tracing lines in the palm. Dr. Robinson Leary and Hadley Joy Morris-Whitfield were leaning forward as far as they could, their elbows on the table, looking first at Mary Rose's hand, then at the gypsy. Every so often Mary Rose said something to the others and they nodded, the gypsy smiled and they stared some more at the upturned palm.

Esmeralda St Benedict was not just a gypsy. She was a *gorgeous* gypsy and both Wiley and Robert focused every so often on her cleavage.

No one asked her age, but she was certainly old enough to be here, in Meadow Lakes Retirement Community. Her hair was black – had to be a really good dye job, and her waistline had thickened a little, but my-oh-my. She was a looker and colorful as a herd of hummingbirds; tall hummingbirds that is, because Esmeralda St Benedict was a little taller than Hadley Joy Morris-Whitfield, and Hadley was still nearly six feet tall.

One evening Hadley had taken the girls to Happy Hollow Country Club and every old dude in the grill and the pub had walked by their table and looked at Esmeralda. What's a girl to do?

Now her companions were laughing and patting Mary Rose on her arms and shoulders. This had gone on for some time and Robert needed to check his prostate into the men's room.

"Be right back," he said to Wiley and he hurried off. He didn't have far to go. This was a retirement community after all and restrooms were just one door outside the dining room.

Wiley Vondra crossed his legs and shook his head. He was long and lean for an old man and when he stood up he looked like a question mark unfolding itself. A hard-working Stetson hat and a brown leather vest were everyday attire. His claim to fame was washing all his clothes at midnight on the 15th of every month in the Meadow Lakes laundry room while butt naked – except for the hat and vest. Frequently the lovely ladies at Table 12 would take afternoon naps on that day, then join him in the laundry room for a few hands of poker.

Wiley Vondra was smiling. He had a thing for Mary Rose McGill, and Mary Rose McGill had a thing right back for Wiley Vondra.

He was still watching as Esmeralda suddenly sat straight up, shoulders back, eyes wide, her face alert and serious as if she were listening to something in the far distance. She jumped up, knocking her chair over behind her.

"We should move away," she said, and in one strong motion she pulled Mary Rose up from her seat, motioned to the others and started to hurry away from the widow. "Move quickly! Come!"

They moved quickly. They came. They scurried after her to a spot a little past where Wiley was seated. He watched this new development like a hawk watches a mouse.

In less than three seconds the huge plate glass window in the dining room smashed to smithereens with an ear-splitting crash. A 1962 pink Cadillac Eldorado convertible flew through the dining room and landed squarely on top of the vacant table 12, where the now splintered and smashed seats were still warm from four female behinds. The convertible top tore off on impact, flew backward out the broken window looking like a giant bat wing, hopped like a deer across the well-groomed lawn and landed in a tulip bed where sprouts were just peeking through the cold ground. A rabbit treating himself to one of the green shoots took off into the trees; tail high, ears standing straight up.

"Frieda!" Hadley yelled, hurrying toward the Cadillac. Steam had started oozing out of its radiator.

"Are you all right?" Robbie Leary yelled and rushed along beside Hadley.

Wiley had jumped up and rushed toward Mary Rose who ignored him and followed the other two women. Wiley took one more step and was standing next to Esmeralda St. Benedict. He put his hands on his hips and together they looked at the car. The Cadillac gave a soft belch. A long, slow sound escaped its tailpipe and sounded like a polite fart. Wiley shook his head. "They don't make 'em like that anymore."

"Theese is true," Esmeralda nodded. "That eez a fine automobile. However, zee 1959 Firebird had the greatest fins of all." They nodded in agreement as the air wheezed out of the Caddy's right front tire.

"Frieda probably has 150,000 miles on that baby," Wiley noted.
Esmeralda agreed again. "At least."

Robbie and Hadley were pulling a short, stocky lady out of the car. She was wearing a purple dress with a wide red belt. One red shoe fell out the driver's door. A large red hat had slipped down over her eyes.

"I can't see!" she said loudly. "Oh, Sweet Lord Above, I can't see!"

Robbie reached up and removed the hat, pulling her hair straight up with it. Now the woman looked like a fright queen on a bad night. Her dress was crooked, her hair stuck straight up, her glasses were hanging from one ear and one shoe was on the dining room floor. She looked mournfully at Hadley. "I think I stepped on the wrong peddle."

Wiley looked over at Esmeralda close by his shoulder. "I had a 1962 Ford Ranchero truck," he grinned. "Advertised: 'Loads of Loadspace' and a 'Luxury Lounge'. Had a black and white interior and I put a necking knob on the steering wheel."

"What eez these….. 'necking nob'?" Esmeralda asked.

Wiley made the shape of a doorknob with one hand and held it up like it was on a steering wheel. "Fastens onto the steering wheel so you have better control. You grab it; steer with your left hand so you can put your other arm around the pretty girl sitting right beside you. None of this power steering and bucket seat stuff."

"That eez a very clever invention!" Esmeralda said, turning her face toward Wiley. They both smiled and nodded in agreement again.

There was a thud and the driver's side door fell off the Cadillac. Water ran down the hood and fell over the big headlights like giant tears.

"That eez a very sad car," Esmeralda said, shaking her head.

Wiley nodded. "Clint Eastwood had a great classic car in that movie, *Gran Torino*."

Esmeralda nudged him with her shoulder. "Wiley Vondra, you are much more man than theese Clint Eastwood. He eez a great actor, but he has zee face like a roadmap."

"Ha!" Wiley snorted. "I've got a face like a prune." He hesitated. "But my stem's still pretty good."

A shout came from the men's room. "Hey! What's going on? I can't get out!" The Cadillac's dramatic entrance had shoved two large tables and four chairs up against the bathroom door.

"Robert's trapped," Wiley said. He moved to the men's room and started lifting chairs and pushing tables away from the door.

"What happened?" Robert asked, seeing the Cadillac as soon as he stepped into the dining room.

"Frieda Grossemouth just dropped in," Wiley said with a smile.

In just a few minutes, Frieda was back in her apartment, quieted down and giving long explanations to Balsac Grossemouth, her aging husband. John, Meadow Lake's general manager had simply gotten into the Cadillac, started the motor and backed it out of the oversized hole in the window. They watched as it limped toward a wrecker waiting in the circular drive in front of Meadow Lakes. Hadley, Robbie and Mary Rose were standing with Wiley, Robert and Esmeralda, watching the action.

Drove that sucker right out to the wrecker," Wiley said.
"Awesome," Robert said.
"Eet is a great car," Esmeralda added. "A great wounded beast."

"I think it looks more like something out of Stephen King," Mary Rose added. "What was the name of his mean car? Carrie? Cujo?"

Robbie smiled. "Carrie was the fire starter, Cujo was the rabid dog. The car was 'Christine'". She looked at Hadley. "Kind of got hung up on 'C' names for awhile there didn't he?" Dr. Robinson Leary, an attractive half Cajun, half black, was also slightly thickened with time. She wore rimless glasses that fit her career. A retired English professor from Creighton University in Omaha, Robbie was keeping up with modern literature by researching and writing a paper on Stephen King. She hoped to make it as horrifying as any one of his books.

Esmeralda smiled. She wore a bright red skirt, a yellow top and had gold hoop earrings. She turned toward the other girls, the bangles on her wrists jangling musically. "All theese excitement makes me want ice cream," she said.

Horses are smart … they know stuff

Ted and Wally's ice cream made the trendy new ice cream store chains look like pikers. Located in a remodeled vintage garage in Omaha's Old Market district, there were four hundred flavors that rotated so you could have the special of the day and hardly repeat yourself in a lifetime. A sign on the ice cream case read, "Children left unattended will be given two shots of espresso and a live puppy."

The girls sat at a table looking out onto Twelfth Street. The sun was setting in the west and long shadows crept through the small windows and crowded around the tables.

Esmeralda took a bite of her honey sesame peanut ice cream. "Robinson, you lived in theese area, am I wrong?"

Robbie motioned toward the north wall with her head. "Right next door in the Mayfair Building."

"Holy Cow," Hadley said. "No pun intended while we're eating ice cream, but we never asked or heard where you lived exactly. We just knew it was in the Old Market."

Robbie nodded again. "It was a great apartment. Cherrywood floors, fireplace, high, high ceilings, exposed brick walls, an interior bedroom with no windows that we called our 'cuddle cave'." She bent over her dish of icy chocolate cheesecake.

"Her husband died there in his sleep," Mary Rose told Esmeralda. "Spooned in bed with her."

"Theese eez a beautiful death," Esmeralda said softly. "You are very fortunate, Robinson."

Robbie nodded and looked up. Her eyes were glistening. "I just couldn't stay afterward. I was afraid and lonely and even though the Old Market is a wonderful community to everyone living here, I decided I wouldn't eat one more meal alone." She looked out the window toward the brick street where a mounted policewoman was riding by on a huge brown horse.

"There are about fifty restaurants in a six block area, and I know servers and managers and owners, but even eating out was eating alone." She took another bite and gave a tiny hiccup.

Hadley reached over and touched her hand. "Grief makes you humble."

"Grief makes you compassionate, too." Mary Rose added.

"And it gives you unchained courage," Robbie sighed. "It took everything I had inside me to make the decision to move to Meadow Lakes, to pack up, to say goodbye to this community and move into an unknown one. Lucky for me, I ended up at Table 12."

Esmeralda was thoughtful. "Grief is a connection of zee soul," she said. "It connects us to all people, for all people grieve. It connects us to The Source. We must be loving and kind to all we meet," she said, "for they are hurting, too."

"How do you mean, 'connects us to The Source?" Mary Rose asked.

Esmeralda gave a little shake of her head, as if coming out of deep thought. She laughed her tinkling, pleasant laugh. "But I am too serious about myself. My great-grandfather was a Sorcerer – one who is connected to The Source or what some call The Great Mystery, The Universe even God. Many things my people do seems like magic to those uneducated in such matters." She put her hand over her heart and smiled an almost magical smile. "Remember girls, I yam gypsy." She turned toward Hadley. "And your man, Hadley; how did he die?"

Hadley dissolved a bite of pumpkin ice cream in her mouth. "Airplane crash. The pilot tried to go through a mountain instead of around it. There wasn't much left to send home to me."

Hadley's husband had been successful in his business. She had been an equally successful professional volunteer who had enjoyed big men, big cars and big dogs. Friends had joked that Hadley had Vidal Sassoon hair after the old ad where the model swung her head and her thick, glamorous hair followed five minutes later. She, too, had thickened with age, but had not lost her height. Her husband, who had not always been the most faithful, was indeed, the most loving and he showed her off like some of his friends showed off their young trophy wives. She had loved him, understood him and created a good life of her own. When she realized she was living in only two rooms of their big house after he was gone, she moved to Meadow Lakes.

She looked at the gypsy seated next to her and smiled. "We go visit our boys every so often." She looked around the table. "They're all buried in the same cemetery and you're welcome to come anytime, Esmeralda."

She glanced over at Mary Rose. "None of our husbands suffered before they died, but Mary Rose's was on life support for a time and that is horridly worrisome."

Mary Rose nodded and, like the others, took a small bite of her ice cream, which happened to be Marble Cake Batter. "He had a stroke during mass one day and died a few days after. Actually my four daughters packed me up and moved me to Meadow Lakes without even talking to me about it. I'm super glad now, but at the time I could have pushed them into the grave with their namby-pamby father." She gave her ice cream dish a glaring look and took a bigger bite.

Mary Rose McGill, sweet Catholic girl and all-round good housewife and mother had taken her fourteen plain, dowdy housedresses, tied one around her two pairs of equally boring shoes, thrown them down the Meadow Lakes garbage chute and proceeded to lose sixty pounds after she met the other BOOB Girls. Now, while Robbie wore jeans and a Creighton Blue Jays sweatshirt, and Hadley had on plain black slacks, white turtleneck and blue jacket, Mary Rose in her lavender pantsuit, red-framed glasses and stylish blonde hair was almost as colorful and Esmeralda St Benedict.

Hadley laughed and pointed her spoon at Mary Rose. "Then she had breast cancer and turned into a tough, one-breasted Amazon." Robbie winked and raised her spoon in salute.

They finished every bite of ice cream. "Now we must walk off theese wonderful calories," Esmeralda said with a sigh. She stood up. "Let us walk across the street to theese Wheatfield's for coffee."

"Not a long walk, but a great destination," Robbie said.

Esmeralda put her arm around Robbie's shoulder as they started out the door. She bent slightly to smile into Robbie's face. "And as we pass your apartment, Robinson, I weel sing a gypsy song to your husband and to your memories."

They stepped outside. Omaha's Old Market was a major tourist attraction with brick streets and wooden awnings dripping multi-colored petunias over the sidewalks in the summer. The old brick buildings were beautiful and now condos and apartments made it the popular place to live in the city. The Missouri river and the pedestrian bridge crossing it were just blocks away. A new stadium hosted the College World Series and when June came the college baseball teams' famous "road to Omaha" led directly to the Old Market's historic streets. From Vivace's fine Italian restaurant, to Hollywood Candy's milk shakes, to talented street musicians and artists, there was always something going on.

Esmeralda led them across the street where they stood and looked up at the majestic Mayfair Building. Built in 1883 as a boot factory, it had produced one thousand boots a day, loaded them on the new railroad and sent them west to cowboys and ranchers on the plains and on through the Rockies to the west coast. Now it boasted twelve fashionable apartments in the heart of the district.

Esmeralda focused her eyes on the fourth floor. Windows nearly ten feet high reflected the last rays of the setting sun. She began to sing. It was a plaintive, sweet song, in a language unknown to them and it brought tears to Robbie's eyes. When Esmeralda was finished, Robbie hugged her and they started down the block and across the street to Wheatfield's, a bakery and restaurant that always emanated good smells.

As they crossed Howard Street a colorful horse-drawn carriage clattered over the bricks, started to turn the corner and then, surprisingly, the horse abruptly changed course and headed straight for Esmeralda. It came to her and stopped, lowering its head to be patted.

The driver jumped down. "Oh man, Lady, I'm sorry! She's never done that before. I tried my damnest to turn her, but she wouldn't stop. Oh crap!" and he grabbed the horse's harness. Esmeralda put a gentle hand on his arm.

"Do not scold theese beautiful animal," she said and she smiled at the driver. "I called her to me."

The girls looked at each other. Esmeralda hadn't done anything of the sort. The horse surprised all of them by walking up to her. Then they watched as the gypsy pulled an apple out of her skirt pocket, gave it to the horse, laid her head against its soft cheek and whispered in its ear. She gave it a several strokes on its long, soft neck, nodded to the carriage driver and backed away, smiling all the while.

The driver relaxed and smiled back. "It's cool," he said. "She likes you. Horses are smart … they know stuff." And he turned the horse and clattered back down the street. Soft carriage bells rang in the fading light.

As they breathed in the sweet smell of fresh baked bread inside the door of Wheatfield's, Robinson Leary had two interesting thoughts. *I don't remember telling her which apartment was ours, but she looked right at it. And just where did that apple come from, anyway?*

Balsac Grossemouth

"SHIT!" Mary Rose McGill said in a voice a little too loud. They were all approaching the dining room just days after Frieda Grossemouth had made her spectacular and dramatic entrance. It wasn't the usual "S" word. The girls used it as their signal to straighten up, literally. It stood for Shoulders back, Head high, Eyes (I) straight ahead and Tummy tucked in. Three years ago Hadley's teenage granddaughter, Paris, had told her Nama that if she kept walking bent over, she would be taller than her grandmother within a year. Hadley had purchased a book on stretching and seen SHIT, which apparently the authors of the book had not noticed they had put into their chapter on posture.

As soon as they heard it, Robbie and Hadley pulled their shoulders back, held up their heads and tucked in their tummies. For old broads, at that moment, they had remarkably good posture. Esmeralda, walking beside them with a wide and charming smile, didn't need SHIT. Her posture was nearly always perfect. She had a perpetual tease of laughter just behind her eyes and it came out as a real and delightful laugh when she put her arm around Mary Rose's shoulder.

"You are so beautiful!" she said. Then she turned back toward Robbie and Hadley. "Eeen all my long life, never have I been so lucky to be weeth such beautiful and remarkable women. I yam grateful."

The first Burned Out Old Broad, the one to name them *THE BOOB GIRLS,* was a short, bow-legged retired rancher from the Nebraska sandhills in the state's long panhandle. She had been saucy, bossy and bold and had led them in a Hummer and trailer to a western town called Resolution. She had personally given them driving lessons so they could all handle the big Hummer and good-sized Jayco trailer. But Maggie Patten had died on a cruise down the west coast. In a raging storm, the other three girls had fastened her suitcase to her body, put a picture of her son in a plastic baggie in her pocket and bravely and dangerously given her the burial at sea she had wanted.

Maggie's chair at Table 12 had been filled shortly after by plain-Jane, boring Patty Whack. But Patty Whack, who had been no fun at all at first, turned out to actually be Calamity Doodles, a ninja-limber spy whose husbands numbers five and six had gone over to the dark side and were out to kill her. She had led the girls in robbing a grave and blowing up a gangster's mansion. Calamity Doodles was a lot more fun than when she was Patty Whack.

Now the fourth seat at Table 12 was being warmed by the attractive behind of this gypsy, Esmeralda St Benedict, about whom the girls knew very little but each felt she had known and loved forever.

They had just finished an afternoon of Stephen King movies which were to provide Robbie with information for her research paper. The Creighton University library had a full collection of King films and the girls were in for several sessions of horrifying movie marathons and a lot of popcorn and sodas.

Hadley had been the devil's advocate and cheered for the jealous car when they watched *Christine* from 1983. "She's one high-octane, tuned-up bitch!" Hadley yelled during one of the 1958 Plymouth Fury's furious rampages. Robbie took copious notes while flipping through pages of the book lying by her side on Hadley's couch. Mary Rose squealed frequently and spent a good deal of time in the bathroom. Esmeralda watched, fascinated.

"Theese eez one truly twisted genius," she said admiringly of King.

"You should read *The Dark Tower* series," Robbie muttered, turning more pages.

The second movie had been *Cujo* and once again Hadley rooted for the rabid not-so-under-dog who is by far the scariest pooch in history. Robbie took more notes and did more muttering, Mary Rose spent even more time hiding in the bathroom and Esmeralda simply said, "Theese dog makes zee Hound of zee Baskervilles look like a tea-cup poodle!"

Now they were headed in for a good dinner together. The window of the dining room had been replaced and Balsac Grossemouth, with genuine Northern European charm and chivalry had seen to the repairs of Frieda's old Cadillac himself, bought her new whitewall tires and a new convertible top and had the car beautifully detailed. It sat now in its parking place at Meadow Lakes, looking proud and beautiful.

If cars had mirrors the Caddy would be holding one by her front tire and admiring herself.

Meadow Lakes Retirement Community was a brick and white three-story building with studio, one and two-bedroom apartments and three luxury apartments boasting three bedrooms. Robbie and Mary Rose were in one-bedrooms, Esmeralda had a small studio apartment and Hadley lived on the top floor in a three-bedroom. One bedroom was hers, one her home office and one for grandchildren who came to visit on rare occasions.

Many people, even senior citizens, tended to think of retirement communities as a home for impeccable decrepitude. Not Meadow Lakes. While there were a few walkers and a couple of scooters parked by the dining room as the girls approached, the residents who enjoyed the three hots and a cot in this community had an age range from 50 to 103 and were all active. Many left each morning for jobs. They joked, laughed and, like all of us, eventually they died.

The girls sat at Table 12 while young servers placed plates of hot breaded salmon, asparagus spears and steamed carrots, along with a generous tossed salad in front of them. There would be pound cake and sherbet for dessert.

"I'm glad this isn't beef or pork," Mary Rose said, taking a bite of her salmon. "I'd be afraid it was Cujo."

Robbie smiled. "I think there were some fish that died in *The Stand.*" She cut an asparagus spear and held it for a minute. "Esmeralda, we don't know much about you, girl. You came just before the holidays and left right after for awhile. Where are you from?"

"I yam Gypsy," Esmeralda said with a smile.

"And that means?" Robbie asked persistently.

"Eeet means I yam of the wandering Roma. We came from Romania," she paused. "Or Turkey or Hungary or Persia. People in Europe, because of zee dark skin, thought we were from Egypt and called us 'gypsies'." She smiled at the girls. "We are wanderers. I have been so many places I do not remember my origins." Robbie ate more asparagus and became thoughtful.

Dr. Robinson Leary was a PhD from Creighton University. She had taught and loved English literature with all her heart, loving only her husband more. He had lived a long and difficult life with multiple sclerosis, spent many years in a wheelchair and had, as Mary Rose said when they were at Ted and Wally's, died quietly in his sleep. Robinson, having heard horrifying rumors of banks locking safety deposit boxes until a will was probated had gotten up from their bed after she realized he was dead, showered, dressed and

before she called anyone, had gone to their
friendly local bank. Since both she and her
husband were African-American, and he made a
stylish figure, even in his wheelchair, the bank
knew them well.

"I need to get into my safety deposit box,
"Robbie had said.

"Sure Doctor Leary," the teller smiled. "Where's
that professor husband of yours?"

Robbie didn't miss a beat. "He's still in bed,"
she said. Robinson Leary was a very practical
woman.

Robbie was of medium height with salt-and-
pepper hair. She wore rimless glasses and while
she, like most older women, had gotten wider,
was still in good shape. Her skin, the color of a
good mocha, was clear and had a handsome
sheen to it. Robinson Leary was content at

Meadow Lakes. She didn't know if she would ever be really happy again, but the BOOB Girls had filled the hole in her heart and she would stay there until she died. Unless she ran out of money.

Robbie had a secret fear of out-living her savings. They had stashed away and invested all they could, but professors didn't make that much, and they had enjoyed their Old Market apartment and eating out at the great restaurants nearby. They had probably enjoyed their money more than they should have, yet she wouldn't change a thing.

Robbie looked at Hadley and smiled. She thought that if worse came to worst and she actually *did* live longer than her money, she could probably sell everything and move into Hadley's third bedroom. She had no children or siblings, just distant cousins in distant places and Hadley, on the other hand, had lots of money.

Hadley was looking at Esmeralda and smiling a soft smile. She had one son who had been married four times now. She saw her three grandchildren at least three times a year – there were birthdays, of course – and she saw her son for lunch every so often. She worried about his divorces and while he was a successful attorney in Omaha, he never seemed happy. During one of their lunches at Mark's Bistro, a trendy place with the best patio in town, he told her something after he'd had two martinis. He had just informed her he was divorcing … again.

"At first, Mother," he said, "I looked for a girl with big ti .. breasts. So I found one, but she had zero passion or personality so I looked for a girl with personality. I found one. She turned out to be a nit-wit who went to pieces every time I looked at another women and passion went out the door after a year. I was moving up in the firm so I decided I wanted a woman with ambition. I found one and her ambition was to be the thinnest woman in the world. Now I'm old enough to have an AARP card and I'm back to looking for a woman with big tits."

Hadley herself had an on-going long-distance relationship with a handsome Native American sheriff she met when Maggie Patten had taken them to the west coast in the Hummer and trailer. Wes Longbow thought Hadley's son, David, to be intelligent, crafty and lonely. Hadley agreed. Now she had a question for Esmeralda.

"But what did your people do, Esmeralda? Did you marry? Have children?"

The gypsy cut off a delicate bite of salmon, stuck her fork into it and then into a steamed carrot. "My people were Lautari, een my language. Musicians. Dancers. And some, as I said, were Sorcerers. For theese marriage; no. Children;no. But *lovers!* Ah, my girlfriends; that eez another story for another time." And she twinkled and grinned a very charming grin.

Mary Rose McGill dug into her salad, "Now *that* I want to hear!"

Mary Rose had four daughters, Mary Claire, Mary Elizabeth, Mary Ruth and Mary Louise. What could she say? She was Catholic. She had been a dutiful wife, an intense mother and never thought of doing anything for herself. That had changed. She was a new woman now, and while her husband hadn't talked to her much while he was alive, she didn't care that he talked to her not at all now that he was dead. Of all of them, Mary Rose was the happiest. She knew the value of life and the value of friends and relished the bond that only women know. Their love for each other had given her a soul.

"We've had a lot of good food and ice cream and popcorn lately," Mary Rose observed. "I'll gain weight unless I do some heavy exercise." She wrinkled her nose and thought for a second. "On the other hand, we all get heavier as we get older. That's because there's a lot more heavy information and knowledge in our heads." They looked at her. She smiled. "That's my story and I'm sticking to it!"

The sherbet and pound cake had just been served when Frieda Grossemouth stood and tapped her glass loudly with her spoon.

"Everyone!" she said. "I want to say something."

She looked around the big dining room and raised her voice. "I want to thank you for all your support during my recent accident. Balsac and I just seem to be accident prone these days. As you know, Balsac is still recovering after his recent bicycle wreck." She looked down and smiled at her husband sitting beside her. "And as many of you know, his scrotum was completely crushed. The pain was excruciating and the doctors didn't know if they could help him."

There was a muffled gasp from the men in the room as they imagined the pain. Wiley Vondra slid down in his chair and whispered, "Sweet Jesus!" to Robert who was sitting beside him.

"Dear God in Heaven," Robert said, touching his Bible. Loretta Ripp, Meadow Lakes' librarian and Robert's special lady, reached over and patted his knee.

"Balsac was unable to hug me or the grandchildren," Frieda went on, "and every move caused him terrible pain." We prayed as the doctors performed a delicate operation, and it turned out they were able to piece together the crushed remnants of his scrotum, and wrap wire around it to hold it in place."

Again, the men cringed and squirmed and Wiley sank even further down in his chair. "I don't believe this," he mouthed to Robert.

"Now," she announced in a quivering voice, "thank the Lord, Balsac is out of the hospital and the doctors say that with time, his scrotum should heal completely."

A few men sighed with relief. There was total silence. Other men actually sat with their bites of pound cake still on their forks poised in front of their gaping mouths. No one moved. Everyone looked at the stately, dignified Balsac Grosse-mouth as he slowly stood. He looked at Frieda with a loving smile and rested his hand on her shoulder. Then he looked out at the frozen crowd before him and smiled. "I just want to remind my dear Frieda," he said with a smile. "The word is *sternum*."

Part Two

On the Road Again

All the girls agreed.

One good thing about growing old was not

having to mess with

The Seven Dwarfs of Menopause

Itchy

Bitchy

Sweaty

Sleepy

Bloated

Forgetful

Psycho

"No one can tell what goes on in between the person you were and the person you become. No one can chart that blue and lonely section of hell. There are no maps of change. You just....come out on the other side ... Or don't." Stephen King, *The Stand*

Stick A Needle in Your Eye

It happened just like that. All of a sudden. No warning at all. It happened just like spring slips into summer in one day – there it is. Hadley got out of bed, grabbed her robe, went into the bathroom, sat on the toilet and pulled her journal out of the drawer under the sink. She had wanted to journal for years and finally found that if she did it, literally first thing in the morning, sitting on the toilet, then she journaled every day. "Might as well do something constructive while you're there," she joked. But this morning something was different ... scary different.

She couldn't see some of the letters she was writing. A granddaughter got her a beautiful new journal every Christmas and there were lovely quotes along the margins of each page, but now Hadley couldn't read the quotes. The letters were crooked. Some were missing. She felt a light sweat break out on her forehead.

"Crap!" she said. Then she looked down at the toilet beneath her. "Sorry. I didn't mean it personally." *CRAP!!* was the only word she wrote in her journal that morning.

She soaked for a time in her big tub and felt tears leaking quietly out of her eyes. "Crap, crap, crap," she whispered. Her grandmother had gone nearly blind from it. Her mother had barely been able to see and wasn't able to read at all. A cousin had been declared legally blind years ago.

She wiped the tears away with a wet hand, splashed water on her face and settled back into her bubbles. "Crap again," she said out loud and she sighed. Tears disappearing in the tub didn't have the same romantic ring that tears disappearing in the rain had. Well, that was life. That was getting old. She gave a little snort. What wasn't broke, hurt. What didn't hurt, leaked and what didn't leak had probably been surgically removed.

She got dressed, dried her hair and put on her makeup, leaning toward the mirror and looking closely at her eyes. Things weren't distorted here. Well, maybe a little. "I will see with my heart, and not just my eyes," she said. And she repeated it. In fact, she repeated it all the way to the dining room where Mary Rose, Robbie and Esmeralda were already waiting at Table 12.

Hadley spoke before she even sat down. "I have macular degeneration," she told them. They looked at her. They were quiet. She sat.

"All the women in my family had it and I thought I'd made it through without getting it, but I had a bleed in my right macular this morning. I can tell."

They were still quiet. Then Robbie pulled out her cell phone. "One of my husband's best friends was a retinal specialist and his son has taken over his practice. He's the one you want to see. If you're a bleed, they work you in the same day you call."

Hadley gave a sad little smile. "I'm a *bleed*," she said

Robbie connected to the Retinal Specialists receptionist, explained why she was calling and turned to Hadley. "One o'clock today okay?" Hadley nodded. Robbie confirmed the appointment and put her phone down.

"Theese is troublesome, Hadley Joy," Esmeralda said, leaning forward. "But take heart, dear one. Your arura eez strong. You weel learn from theese and become a stronger, wiser woman."

Hadley shook her head. "Can't I just stay a stupid wimp and not have it at all?"

Mary Rose shook her head. "You are a survivor Hadley. Tell Esmeralda what you said to your OB-GYN when he did your uterine biopsy."

Eight years ago Hadley had been diagnosed with uterine cancer, undergone surgery and had gotten three quick radiation treatments.

Hadley smiled a more genuine smile this time. "He was the world's cutest OB-GYN," she said to Esmeralda, leaning forward toward the gypsy. "I was there on *the table* with my legs in the stirrups and he pulled the biopsy tube out. It looked really good and he said, 'Fantastic!' I said, 'Do you know what it means to a lady my age to have a handsome young man look between her legs and say, 'Fantastic?'"

Esmeralda threw back her head, clapped her hands and laughed her magical laugh. The others joined in, including Hadley.

Hadley looked thoughtful. "Of course it wasn't fantastic, it was cancer. But I really did come through it stronger and wiser and now I can actually say it was a good experience for me."

Robbie formed her hand into a pistol and pointed it at Hadley. "Okay, girlfriend, if macular degeneration is ARMD – that's Age Related Macular Degeneration for most people, but for you, Babe, it means Armed and Dangerous." Hadley laughed again. "Thank you, Ladies," she said, standing up. "I feel better. Let's hit that buffet before it gets cold."

They hit the buffet. It wasn't cold.

The Waiting Room

Dr. Edward McGillacudy's office was in one of the tall medical towers next to one of Omaha's even taller hospitals. Hadley had dressed well to see her new doctor. She learned early on when she volunteered at one of the hospitals that people who look nice, neat, well-dressed and important get better treatment no matter how hard the staff tries to treat everyone equally well. Husband hospitalized? The well-dressed visiting wife can ask where the secret coffee pot is located and be taken to it; others are directed to the cafeteria. She wore a black pin-stripe pantsuit with a grey turtleneck and black shoes with medium high heels. A black necklace with a silver charm hung around her neck. With her grey hair, she was very attractive.

Robbie went with her and drove the Hummer. She too, was dressed nicely. After all, her husband had more than his share of doctor visits and there was one more factor entering into

Robbie's selection of wardrobe. She was black, and because of it made an extra effort to dress well. Without having talked about it, Robbie wore a black pantsuit, white turtleneck and black medium high heels.

"We either look like salt and pepper Bobbsey Twins or two funeral directors out recruiting business," Robbie said when they met at eleven.

"For this," Hadley replied, "I'm opting for the funeral directors."

They planned to drive to The Old Market, have spinach salad at M's Pub and put a good face on Hadley's doctor's visit. Robbie had reasoned that the least they could do would be to show Dr. Ed that Hadley could eat spinach without getting any in her teeth.

M's was a classic Old Market eatery. Hadley always thought it was like walking into a good place in New York City. The walls were brick; the big circular bar was marble-topped and held a massive, towering bouquet of professionally arranged live flowers. Lighting was soft and perfect and if you could get a table by the floor-to-ceiling front windows, you had a choice view of Old Market activity.

Robbie had called ahead. Their server sat them near the window. In just a few minutes the manager hurried over. Robbie stood up, got a warm hug, introduced Hadley and said that yes, since she hadn't been in for so long, they would love a complimentary glass of wine.

Hadley was sure she couldn't eat anything, but after one bite of the salad, with its warm dressing with just the right amount of bacon and spice, she was sunk. She dug in.

Robbie looked at her and grinned. "Remember how we say, 'When have you ever heard someone say, *I'm stressed! Let's go have salad.'?"* Hadley had just forked more spinach than she should have. She grinned back, opened wide and stuck it all in. "Ummmmmmm." And she nodded. It was great comfort food.

M's atmosphere was better anytime than any doctor's office, even though the Retinal Specialists had a reasonably cozy waiting room. It was a long, L-shaped affair, with receptionists behind a large counter at one end. A row of small, high windows lined one wall, catching the afternoon sun. Hadley took a deep breath and noticed, unintentionally, that at least it didn't *smell* like a doctor's office.

There were ten other people sitting in chairs, waiting to be called. Hadley glanced around and decided that there were five patients ahead of her. Everyone had had to have someone drive them there. Getting your eyes dilated wasn't all that conducive to long road trips. Plus, half those sitting had magazines or books in front of them. The non-reading patients might as well have had big signs around their necks saying, "It's me."

They sat under the row of windows and both reached for a magazine at the same time. Hadley laid hers on her lap, unopened. "I hate this," she whispered.

"Me, too," Robbie whispered back.

"What if he gives me meds? I hate meds."

"Ask him if he'll give you a prescription for margaritas."

Hadley looked at her and smiled. ""Does that come with a medical warning?"

Robbie smiled back and pointed a finger at Hadley.

"Do you have feelings of inadequacy? Do you suffer from shyness? Do you sometimes wish you were more assertive? Do you suffer exhaustion from the day-to-day grind? If you answered yes to any of these questions, ask your doctor about **Margaritas.**"

Hadley thought for a second. "Margaritas may not be right for everyone. Women who are pregnant or nursing should not use Margaritas."

Robbie picked it up, " However, women who *wouldn't mind* nursing or becoming pregnant are encouraged to try it, being mindful that side effects may include …" she pointed her finger back at Hadley, who looked at the ceiling.

"Dizziness. Nausea. Incarceration. Erotic lustfulness. Loss of clothing." Robbie touched her arm and interrupted her. "Loss of money. Loss of virginity. Table dancing." She paused. "And a desire to sing Karaoke."

Robbie turned in her seat to face her friend. "The consumption of Margaritas may make you think you are whispering when you are not.

The consumption of Margaritas may cause you to tell your friends over and over again that you love them. The consumption of Margaritas may make you think you can logically converse with members of the opposite sex."

They looked at each other and did a high five.

A man sitting two chairs left of Hadley leaned forward. "You ladies do anything with Jack Daniels?"

The Dark Man Cometh

The door to the waiting room opened. A husky young woman in jeans and a University of Nebraska Cornhuskers sweatshirt was struggling to push a very large woman in a wheelchair through the door. Her shirt had the famous skull and crossbones in a football helmet that marked the symbol of the team's Blackshirt Defense. When a defensive player did a good job, he was

awarded a black shirt. The young woman looked
as if she had earned hers.

The lady in the chair was squeezed into it. And
while it was cool outside, this patient wore a
jacket much too heavy for the weather. A wool
cap covered her head and sweatpants and boots
covered her legs. She was wearing mittens and
dabbing her eyes with a man's handkerchief. She
didn't look at anyone through her watering eyes.
She just stared straight ahead as if she were
totally blind, which Hadley thought entirely
possible.

It was hard not to look at her. Hadley noticed
Robbie was fiddling with her wedding ring,
looking down at her hands. The young woman
parked the wheelchair and its occupant in a
corner, went to the counter and signed in, then
she came back and sat down beside the older
woman. She grabbed a magazine without

speaking and started to read. The older woman continued to blankly look straight ahead.

In just a few minutes the same door opened again. Another wheelchair rolled slowly in. This time a woman about their age came alone through the door and wheeled up to the counter. She spoke to the nurse, signed in, then wheeled to a spot against the wall. Hadley watched her.

She, too, was heavy in a flat, flabby way, but her hair was beautiful; shoulder length, thick, grey-ing-blonde and it shone under the light. The most noticeable thing, though, was the one leg clothed in a gray slack. There was only one. *Diabetic?* Hadley imagined. She turned to Robbie.

"I know why we talk so much about our illnesses when we grow older," she said in a soft voice. "It becomes all-consuming."

Robbie nodded. "I think that whenever we have dinner at Table 12 or anywhere else, Death and Grief come sit with us and have a dry martini." She paused and smiled. "But for a real gross-out, here's how Stephen King described Randall Flagg, his Devil in *The Stand.* It was in a part he called, *The Dark Man Cometh."* She grinned a wicked grin, leaned toward Hadley and whispered, *"He was a clot looking for a place to happen, a splinter of bone hunting a soft organ to puncture, a lonely lunatic cell looking for a mate..."*

Hadley interrupted her. "Robinson Leary! This Stephen King thing is spooky! Can't you research Mari Sandoz or some other nice writer from Nebraska?"

Robbie grinned her wicked grin again. "Nope. Stephen King is the master, and what I quoted, girlfriend? That's *wordsmithing*." She opened her eyes wide, stuck out her tongue and wiggled her fingers in front of her face. Just then a cheery voice called out.

"Hadley?" An attractive, white haired woman was smiling and looking at them. "Come with me, please."

"The dark man cometh," Robbie whispered. She grinned and followed her friend.

The woman's nametag read, "Carla" and she led Hadley and Robbie into a small room with a small desk, two chairs, the ever-present eye chart and a poster showing a retina.

I like puppy posters better, Hadley thought, looking it over.

"I'm going to dilate your eyes, Hadley, then we'll take a look at the chart on the wall." Carla was pleasant, had a great smile and now that things were started, Hadley felt a little better.

They'd be out of here soon and back to safe and cozy Table 12. Robbie stood against the wall with her arms folded.

The drops weren't bad. Carla gave Hadley tissues to wipe away any drips then gave her a small, decorative little thing to hold over one eye while she looked at the chart on the wall. She could read several lines down with her left eye, but could hardly get by the big E with her right. A small shiver of panic ran through her body.

Carla smiled. "I gotta tell you. A long time ago I worked in an office where we just had folks hold one hand over one eye and read with the other eye. There was one man who came in, I said, 'Cover your left eye with your left hand and read for me.' He did. Then I said, 'Now cover your right eye with your right hand and read again.' He did. Then I said, "Now with both." Nothing. He didn't say a word. Well, when I looked, sure enough, instead of reading with both eyes, he'd

covered his eyes with *both hands.* " Hadley gave
a polite little laugh as a pretty redhead came to
the doorway, smiled and asked them to follow
her.

Tarah was perky and bright and somehow made
everything she was doing just seem right and
normal. Hadley thought she had a perfect
personality to be a tech in a doc's office;
pleasant, not overbearing and didn't talk down to
them or treat them like women old enough to be
her mothers, or maybe even her grandmothers.

She led them to another room and sat Hadley
down in front of a machine that would take
pictures of her retinas. "Blink," Tarah said.
"Now don't blink, Hold. Hold. Hold." A line,
which looked like a long squiggle to Hadley, but
which she was pretty sure was pretty straight,
went down, down, down the screen in front of
her.

Tarah stood, smiled and led them to still another room. "Won't be long now," she smiled. "As soon as you're dilated Doctor will see you. You'll like him."

"Ain't technology grand?" Robbie smiled.

"Be quiet," Hadley said back to her. "I'm listening to my pupils expand." They waited. Her pupils expanded.

Dr. Edward McGillacudy

Cute as a bug, Hadley thought when Ed McGillacudy walked through the door. No white coat. No annoying stethoscope hanging around his neck. He wore a nice but not terribly expensive business suit, a Creighton BlueJay tie and had a blonde burr cut. His eyes twinkled and when he saw Robbie he stopped, put his hands on his hips and said, "Dr. Leary!"

Robbie smiled a big smile. "Dr. McGillacudy!"

They hugged. He was about Robbie's height, which made him just a little shorter than Hadley, but he gave off a large, confident presence and Hadley immediately liked him. He was open, relaxed and she thought how it was probably neat having him for a boss. Or a son.

Hadley was sitting in a big chair with headrest and arms and a footrest. There were tissues and swabs and more posters of eyes and the usual beige paint on the walls.

"Ok," the doctor said, getting down to business. "Hadley," and he reached out to shake her hand. But Hadley, sitting in his big chair, opened her arms for a hug and got one as big as the one Robbie had received. "Here's what we have." He put the photos Tarah had taken into a computer and showed them to Hadley and Robbie. "Here's your bleed and see this swelling? Goes with the territory." He looked as her chart Carla had completed. "When your mother had this, there was nothing we could do. But in the last ten years there have been tremendous advances. We can help this a lot with just a shot in the eye now and then."

"*A shot in the eye?!*" Robbie and Hadley said it together and loud enough so that two people sitting across the hall looked up, smiled at each other and nodded knowingly.

Ed McGillacudy smiled, too. "Not as bad as it sounds. We numb your eye and all you feel is a little pinch." He thought for a second then touched Hadley's hand ever so gently. "It does give a whole new meaning to 'stick a needle in your eye', though."

"*A shot in the eye?*" They said it together again, but not as loud this time. Dr. Ed chuckled and patted Hadley's shoulder.

She looked up at him from her seat in the big

chair. "I saw that on *House*, the TV show once. The needle was about two feet long."

"Not this one," Ed said. He picked up a small needle, unwrapped it and showed her. "It just goes under the first layer of your eye, cuts off the blood flow and reduces the swelling. Your vision should improve dramatically. I know it sounds scary. I've had 300-pound football players faint when they've had to have a steroid shot in their eye." He patted Hadley again. "OK, let's do this. It only takes a second. Want to lay back for me?"

"Frankly, no," Hadley said. Dr. McGillacudy reclined her chair a little anyway.

"This is the worst part," he said as he put a retractor around her eye so she wouldn't blink.

No it's not, Hadley thought. She caught a glimpse of Robbie standing with her arms crossed, eyes wide, mouth open, watching.

Dr. Ed swabbed Hadley's eye with some blessed numbing solution, took the needle in his hand, leaned over her and said as softly as if he were talking to a child, "On three. One – two –," and on two the needle went in. Hadley felt a tiny prick and saw a wash of liquid move toward the back of her eye.

"That wasn't so bad," she whispered. Then there was a roar like a freight train, she had a wave of weakness and everything went black.

Hadley Joy Morris-Whitfield, dignified and worldly, had fainted dead away.

A Terrible, Awful, Bad, No Good Day

Hadley was lying on her couch, a cold wet wash cloth over her eyes, a quilt over her legs and middle. Robbie had just pulled up a chair to sit beside her when Esmeralda hurried in the door, carrying a little box.

"How did eet go?" she asked, pulling up a footstool which made her on an eye level with Hadley's covered-up eyes.

"She took it like a 300-pound football player," Robbie said.

Esmeralda looked puzzled. Robbie smiled. "She fainted."

"Pitiful!" Hadley moaned. "I was pitiful. How did it go? It was humiliating, embarrassing, *pitiful.*

"I meant zee shot," Esmeralda said.

Robbie looked at her. They hadn't mentioned that Hadley had gotten a shot. Before she could ask how Esmeralda knew there had been a shot in the eye involved, Hadley spoke up,

"Oh the shot was nothing at all. No big deal. But

I have to have a series of them and what if I faint every time? He might as well just shoot me on a table so I'll get a little rest out of the whole thing."

Esmeralda reached over and patted Hadley's hand. "Hadley Joy. Eet is not good to wallow een self-pity." She smiled and shrugged, "But eet doesn't hurt to put your feet een and swish them around a leetle."

She gentle removed the washcloth from Hadley's eyes. "Here. Seet up. I brought you a geeft."

Hadley sat up and Esmeralda handed her the little box. Robbie noticed her accent seemed a little heavier than usual.

"That's nice of you, Esmeralda." Hadley opened the box. Inside was a white eye patch. There was an outline of a feminine eye drawn on the front with a blue jewel in the center for the eyeball and long fake eyelashes surrounding it. The edge of the patch was embroidered with sequins and rhinestones. It was comical and beautiful at the same time. Hadley laughed, put it on and hurried into the bathroom to look into the mirror.

"This is terrific!" Her voice coming from the bathroom was light and happy again. "But where's Mary Rose? She should see this."

The gypsy looked at the floor for a second. "Mary Rose eez having a terrible, awful, bad, no good day." They were frozen in place. Mary Rose had done so well after her cancer. Had she found another lump? Hadley came rushing out of the bathroom, eye patch in place and hair brushed. She sat on the edge of the couch. Robbie leaned forward in her chair. Esmeralda went on. "Just as you left she had a call from her oldest daughter."

"Mary Claire," Hadley and Robbie said together.

"Theese is correct. Mary Claire is getting a divorce."

Hadley and Robbie breathed sighs of relief and all three jumped up as Mary Rose walked through the door Esmeralda had left open.

"I can see you heard," she said softly, and she moved toward them for a hug.

"I've been on the phone all afternoon with my other girls and the grandchildren. It's a fifty-fifty verdict. Half of them are devastated and half say they should have done it years ago."

"How about you, Mary Rose?" Hadley asked. "How do you feel?"

"I'm in the devastated column," Mary Rose sighed. "I didn't know things were bad. And I love my son-in-law." She had obviously been crying and now tears sprang to her eyes again.

"I always thought if I ever ended up alone and really needed help, he would be the one I could call anytime and he'd be there to fix whatever needed fixing."

"Hey. You still can," Robbie said. "One of my colleagues at the university had two daughters who divorced. Every year she had a FSIL lunch with the boys. Stands for Former Sons-In-Law." She looked at Mary Rose and was very serious. "Just because a relationship dies, it doesn't mean love dies, too."

Mary Rose nodded. "And I don't want them to live into old age being miserable."

"Ah." Hadley said. "I heard about a couple in their nineties who went to a divorce attorney and said they wanted a divorce. He said, 'My God. You're in your nineties. How long have you been married?' The husband said, 'Seventy five long, miserable years.' The attorney looked at the wife and said, 'Why in the world didn't you divorce years ago?' She looked back at him. 'We wanted to wait 'till all the children were dead."

They chuckled. "Well, all their children are *grown*," Mary Rose said. "And their children represent the fifty-fifty thing. One devastated, one relieved." She squared her shoulders. "And I'm proud of me!" She looked at them. "In my old life I would have wailed and said, "How could you do this to me? But now I know this isn't about me. It's about *them,* and my job is to give them both love and support and let them know I care about them."

She looked at Hadley. "Cool patch. How'd it go?"

"She fainted," Robbie and Esmeralda said together.

"There eez only one thing to do to end such a

terrible, awful, bad, no good day." Esmeralda announced. "Instead of dinner here at Meadow Lakes, we must go to zee Ted and Wally's for ice cream."

Their day wasn't over yet. Small, good things, including ice cream, were yet to come.

You Never Can Tell When You'll Meet A Midget

"I scream, you scream, we all scream for ice cream!" Mary Rose sang it out as they brought their dishes of ice cream, syrups, nuts and whipped cream to a cozy table at Ted and Wally's. The Old Market was beginning its evening bustle and people were coming in and out the old doors, laughing and making major flavor decisions.

Esmeralda looked at the different dishes sitting hopefully in front of her friends. "Ah. Did you know zee ice cream you pick tells us much about zee personality of she who eats it?" They looked at her and all took their first bite at the same time. "I shall bless you weeth a reading." She leaned forward.

"Mary Rose. You picked zee wonderful butter pecan. Theese means you are zee perfect worker, respectful, thoughtful, and devoted with zee very strong sense of right and wrong." The girls looked at Mary Rose and nodded.

"Ah, Robinson. You are indeed zee double chocolate chunk; lively, kind, extremely intelligent and creative. Plus zee beauty of zee chocolate complements your beautiful skin." They all looked at Robbie and nodded again.

"And, Hadley." They all turned toward Hadley who was still proudly wearing her eye patch even though it was no longer needed. "You have chosen zee rich, exciting Rocky Road. Theese tells us you are adventuresome, a risk taker, an adventurer. You are determined, secure and," Esmeralda smiled a big smile and patted Hadley's arm, "aggressive and flirtatious."

"Whooooo EEE!" Mary Rose said as a cozy little blush crept up Hadley's cheeks.

"So what does vanilla with lots of nuts mean?"

The voice came from between Mary Rose and Robbie's shoulders. Standing just behind them was a grinning midget dressed in a red jogging suit and wearing red women's wedgies.

"Clyde!" Hadley, Robbie and Mary Rose yelled together and they jumped up from their chairs.

"'For Pete's sake, sit down!" the midget said. "I can hug you better when you're sitting. Otherwise I develop a relationship with your midsections."

"Cool eye patch," he said as he hugged Hadley. "Get a shot in the eye?"

He looked at Esmeralda and grinned. "Hi Beautiful. Remember me?"

Clyde had once lived at Meadow Lakes with his three brothers (different fathers), Robert, Rueben and Leonard. They had called themselves The BOOB Boys – the Burned Out Old Bastards. Robert, the retired minister still lived in the retirement community with Loretta Ripp, the librarian. Rueben had died of pneumonia and Leonard had run off to join the circus with their last BOOB Girl, Calamity Doodles, former circus performer and retired spy.

Now Clyde and his aunt, Evangeline Goldberg, lived in a small duplex they had purchased together. The backyard was beautifully fenced and designed as a playground for several little dachshunds Clyde had rescued from a gangster's mansion just before Calamity had blown it to high heaven after retrieving a hidden microchip.

At one time they had each cared for one of the little wiener hounds, but Clyde's love for them and their love for him had allowed them to give them up when he told them about his dreams of a duplex and yard. Now only Wylie Vondra had one of the small badger chasers. Ladybug, who was totally blind, would not leave Wylie's side.

Clyde pulled up a chair and climbed up. "I came to get a gallon of ice cream to go with Aunt Evangeline's cinnamon rolls and treated myself with a plain vanilla sundae. What's that say about me, Esmeralda?"

The gypsy put her arm around Clyde's shoulders and squeezed him. "Ah, Clyde. Vanilla eez anything but plain. Eet says you are solid, dependable, straightforward and tremendously compassionate. You are zee good friend everyone needs." She smiled at him. "And you love zee doggies." She looked at the mounds of nuts topping each of their dishes. "Zee nuts – they speak for themselves."

"You can be of great help," Esmeralda said to him. "We need to get away. We need, as my wandering family would tell us; 'find our true north.' And I believe far north of here and far west eez a vonderful place called Camp Robinson, just like zee beautiful Robinson Leary." She pointed a finger with a bright red nail at Robbie and winked.

Robbie grinned and pointed back. "How did you know that is where we hoped to go this Summer, Esmeralda? And how did you know the old Indian fort used to be called *Camp* Robinson before it was *Fort* Robinson?"

Esmeralda smiled, shrugged and patted Clyde's shoulder. "I yam gypsy,' she said.

The life I love is making music with my friends, and I just can't wait to get on the road again. (Willie Nelson)

They were going to Fort Robinson. They were excited. They planned to eat breakfast at Meadow Lakes then drive to Shoemaker's Truck Stop near Lincoln, Nebraska. There, among decorative antique gas pumps, they would order one piece of homemade pie with ice cream and four forks. After that, they would travel beautiful Nebraska Highway 2 across the state to Fort Robinson, the jewel of Northern Plains Indian Forts, nestled into the long Nebraska panhandle.

The road would take them past Chimney Rock and somewhat along the trail of the wagons that had headed west more than a century ago. They would find a campground before dark and enjoy an evening of relaxation. The movie of choice, of course, would be a Stephen King to help Robbie complete her research paper. Mary Rose had already decorated the bathroom in the trailer for a stylish, comfortable, designated hiding place during the really scary parts.

They had laughed and planned all through breakfast. It was a good start to a good day. They had gone to their apartments as soon as breakfast was over to finish any last-minute packing that waited for them.

Hadley Joy Morris-Whitfield went straight to her bathroom, looked in her mirror, brushed her hair back behind her ear and peered at her reflection. There was not as much distortion in her right eye now. The shot seemed to be working. She would get a second one when they got back and she dreaded it every single day; every time she thought of it, actually. She said four words out loud to the image in the mirror. "Grace. Humor. Courage and Confidence." She smiled.

Some time ago a speaker had come to Meadow

Lakes and talked about the importance of positive self-talk. She had encouraged everyone to choose four power words to live by and to say them over and over several times a day. They had laughed about them over breakfast, shared them with Esmeralda and laughed again as she struggled to find her four power words.

"Grace. Humor. Courage and Confidence." Hadley said them again in a sing-song voice as she folded a sheet of paper and stuck it in the side of her purse sitting on the bed next to her suitcase, ready to get on the road again.

Dr. Robinson Leary was looking in her mirror at the same time. "Curiosity. Bravery. Growth and Hope." She frowned at her wrinkles, touched up her lipstick, went into her bedroom and sat a bag filled with four Stephen King books and four Stephen King movies on the bed beside her suitcase and small black teddy bear. The bear's paws held recordings of the voices of her mother and husband. Where Robinson Leary went, her teddy bear went also.

Mary Rose McGill smiled into her mirror and said, "Faith. Trust. Compassion. Independence." Then she made the sign of the cross, cleaned her red-framed glasses, pulled a Coldwater Creek catalog from a drawer under her sink, lifted the toilet seat, pulled down her slacks and pink panties and sat down.

Esmeralda St Benedict had chosen four words all right. She had told the girls her words would be "Love. Care. Spirit and Support." But when her dark eyes took in her image in the mirror of her small bathroom it reflected her placing her left hand on her right shoulder, her right hand on her left shoulder, forming a cross over her chest. She bowed her head and said different words in a language her friends would never know or understand. Then the gypsy said, "Now we begin." She turned and walked out the door of her studio apartment, suitcase in tow, to meet her friends by the fireplace in the lobby.

Everyone but Mary Rose was right on time.

Robbie looked at her watch. "She's ten minutes late."

Hadley looked at her watch, pulled out her cell phone and speed-dialed Mary Rose's number. After five rings Mary Rose's voice invited her to leave a message. Hadley ended the call. "We might as well go have a cup of coffee," she said. She turned to Esmeralda. "I imagine she's in the bathroom. Ever since her chemotherapy she's had bouts of constipation and she tries to poop every morning right after breakfast."

Esmeralda nodded. "Theese can be most annoying for the pooper."

The three of them headed into the tasteful little

Meadow Lakes bistro, got coffee and sat at one of the white tables. They waited. And waited.

Hadley tried Mary Rose again. No answer. "You think we should go check on her?" Robbie asked, just as Mary Rose came rushing around the corner. She sat her suitcase alongside the others the girls had left in the lobby.

"I'm sorry. I was pooping." She sat down and pulled out her phone.

"Mary Rose! Come on!" Hadley said. "We're already an hour late starting. For Pete's sake don't call anybody!"

Mary Rose looked at her. "I'm not calling anybody. I have to fill in my PoopLog before I get in the Hummer. I get car sick if I try to do it while I'm riding."

"PoopLog?" Robbie and Hadley said together.

Esmeralda leaned forward, looked at Mary Rose's phone and smiled.

"Look at this," Mary Rose said. "It's wonderful. It's an application," she turned toward Esmeralda. "They're called 'apps'. This one shows what your poop is telling you."

"Your poop talks to you?" Robbie said.

Mary Rose ignored her. She turned the phone toward the others. "See these little brown dots in the first picture? Those say you're constipated. You need more fiber and water. This next little picture that looks like a dark puddle? That's diarrhea and you need to look into that. Probably means you ate something you shouldn't have or you're stressed. Here's the one you want. It looks like a snake." They looked.

"Your poop should look like a snake." Hadley said with a quick eye roll.

Mary Rose showed them the app on the front of her phone. The icon for PoopLog looked like a Hershey's kiss without the wrapper.

"That is truly gross." Hadley said.

"You actually keep track of your poop?" Robbie asked.

"Theese, what you call it? *Technology*," Esmeralda said, a note of awe coming through her voice. "Theese *technology* eez wonderful."

Mary Rose smiled a small smile of victory, shut off her phone and led them out the door to the Hummer which was waiting patiently in the parking space next to Frieda Grossemouth's pink Cadillac. The two big vehicles made a good looking couple.

Jewish Mothers

Robbie turned the Hummer and trailer onto
Nebraska Highway 2 after a coffee stop in Grand
Island, a little city the Platte River had actually
turned into an island. The pie had been delicious
in Lincoln. The coffee was fine in Grand Island
and the four friends had driven in comfortable
silence and in delightful laughter along the way.

After a few minutes, Hadley pulled out the sheet
of paper tucked into her purse. "My good Jewish
friend, Netta, in Boston loves Jewish mother
jokes and she emailed me this." She opened the
paper. "OK, I'm going to read the first line, you
three see if you can be a Jewish mother and
finish with the second line." She cleared her
throat and adjusted the reading glasses she had
pulled out of her purse.

"What would Mona Lisa's Jewish mother say?"
Hadley grinned and they all thought for a
minute. Then Mary Rose bounced up and down

in her seat up front by Robbie.

"I've got it! I've got it! 'All the money your father and I spent on braces, this you call a smile?'" They all laughed.

"Christopher Columbus' mother." Hadley read. They thought again. Robbie opened her mouth but Mary Rose beat her.

"I don't care what you discovered. You didn't call or write." Mary Rose clapped her hands.

Hadley read on down the list. "OK, Mary Rose, try this one. Michelangelo's mother."

Hadley looked up and smiled at Mary Rose, who put her hand to her head like Johnny Carson used to do and said, "You only painted the ceiling? Why can't you do walls like the other mother's children?"

No one was even trying to guess now. Mary Rose was on a roll.

"Thomas Edison's mother?"

"OK, it's good you invented the electric light bulb, now turn it off and go to bed. Do you know what that thing's going to cost us every month?"

"Albert Einstein's mother?"

"You get a professional photograph taken and you can't do something with your hair?"

"How about Moses' mother?"

Esmeralda, riding in the back seat with Hadley, held up her hand. "Theese I know! Theese I know! She would say, 'Dessert schmesert. Where have you really been for forty years?"

Mary Rose turned and pointed her finger at

Esmeralda. "And you never even called me!"

"Here's a tough one," Hadley said. "Bill Gate's Jewish mother."

They all thought for a second, then Robbie and Mary Rose said together, "It would have killed you to become a doctor?"

"I get to say the last one myself," Hadley said. "Bill Clinton's Jewish mother says, 'Well, at least she was a nice Jewish girl, that Monica.'"

Now, with steaming cups of coffee on a table in front of them, looking out at the 18-wheelers in the small truck stop they had found in an equally small town, Hadley ordered another piece of pie and four forks to celebrate the fun they'd had so far. "When I get my fatal diagnosis," she said. "I'm going to Wheatfields and buy at least three pies. I'm going to just have pie for every meal. I plan to kill whatever I have with sugar.'"

"Call us, we'll join you," Robbie and Mary Rose said together.

Robbie put a piece of fresh blueberry sweetness in her mouth and said, "So Esmeralda. How did you figure out the Moses' mother line?"

Esmeralda smiled. "I yam gypsy. Eet was my ancestors who were wandering around weeth Moses." She smiled her sly, twinkly smile. "I'm sure my great-great and more greats grandmother seduced him. At least she would have tried."

"Mary Rose, you really did well. You figured them all out," Robbie said.

"I should have," Mary Rose replied with a big grin. "Hadley forwarded them to me as soon as she got the email from Netta."

Highway 2

Most people crossing Nebraska take Interstate 80. It's straight, flat and fast. Most have no idea that just north of the interstate is Highway 2, which Charles Kuralt named as one of the ten most beautiful highways in America and which is now listed as a national scenic drive.

There are 20,000 square miles of beautiful sandhills in the upper fourth of Nebraska. Every year over one million wildfowl, including hundreds of thousands of Sandhill Cranes migrate over the great Platte River waterway, drawing birders from around the world. A statue at the Omaha airport celebrates the mating dance of the cranes and Crane Coffee shops are an Omaha chain.

The Platte River, known as a mile wide and a foot deep, kept pioneers alive on their trek west. Some claim they crossed it as many as thirteen times on their way to the Rocky Mountains.

The scenery showed the travelers inside the Hummer native prairie grasses. A trio of deer bounded across the road as the afternoon waned. Farm machinery looked like skeletal dinosaurs against the setting sun and in every colorful small town there was a local restaurant named after the woman who owned it.

"We should have waited until we found Elsie's Café to get our last pie," Robbie said.

That's when the right rear tire of the Hummer blew, sending a blast like a shotgun through the big truck – on the longest and loneliest stretch of beautiful Nebraska Highway 2.

Mysterious Bells

"Crap – Crap – **Crap!**" Hadley said, every "Crap" getting louder. Robbie had pulled off the two-lane highway onto the wide dirt shoulder. They stood on the passenger side of the car, arms on their hips, looking at a miserably flat tire.

"I'll call Hummer Road Service," Hadley said. She pulled out her phone. "CRAP again! There's no cell phone service here!"

"Probably wouldn't do much good." Robbie shook her head. "I doubt out-state Nebraska has a heck of a lot of Hummer dealers."

A massive coal train whizzed by beside them, the tracks running parallel to the highway. There were over 150 train cars zooming by them, headed east to light up Chicago. The coal trains had been their companions since they left Grand Island, but they were no help now.

"Somebody will come by and stop and help us," Mary Rose smiled with too-perky confidence. "After all, this is the country. People help each other here."

Esmeralda didn't say anything. The gypsy just walked a few yards in front of the Hummer, stood with her hands across her chest as she had done while looking in the mirror before they left, and stared north over the railroad tracks into the fields where a gravel road crossed the tracks and joined the highway near where they were stranded.

No cars passed them. The sun was setting with only about a half hour of light left.

"Look," Mary Rose said. She pointed a little way west and across the highway. A small herd of fat Angus cows had come to their fence and were lined up staring at the women. "Omaha Steaks."

"Well, Hadley said. "At least there's a bathroom in the trailer and if worse comes to worst, we can sleep in there without the slides out."

Time dragged on. They leaned against the Hummer. Mary Rose climbed into the trailer and went to the bathroom. They looked at Esmeralda.

"What do you think she's doing?" Robbie asked.

"Wanting to be alone? Meditating?" Hadley guessed. The sun had set and now the light of dusk was beginning to wane, too.

"Listen!" Robbie said, reaching out and touching Hadley's arm.

The pleasant sound of small, tinkling bells was approaching them from the road Esmeralda was watching.

"Bells?" Mary Rose asked, clambering out of the trailer.

"They sound like the ones on the horses in the Old Market." Robbie said.

They turned and looked toward the old farm road. Esmeralda hadn't moved. She was focused on the road, a lovely, quiet smile on her lips.

"I can't see anything," Mary Rose said. "But those are as clear as, well hey, clear as a bell."

In just a few minutes a wagon pulled by two beautiful black horses came into view.

"Help!" Mary Rose yelled, jumping up and down. "Help!"

Hadley smiled. "I think they see us."

"They're using horses," Robbie said. "Amish? I didn't know there were any Amish in Nebraska." Esmeralda walked toward the horses as they moved onto the shoulder in front of the Hummer, shaking their heads and prancing. The gypsy walked to the horses and laid her head against one massive black neck. Robbie could see that she was smiling and her eyes were closed.

Two men in farm overalls, flannel shirts, heavy boots and straw hats moved toward the Hummer.

"We had a bit of a flat," Hadley said. They ignored her, got the spare out of its compartment and expertly began to change the tire. Robbie moved forward and peered around into the face of the young man nearest her.

"Thank you for doing this." She was looking at an unlined face, framed in hair as black as the cargo on the coal trains. The older of the men, black hair streaked with grey, was positioning the spare, ready to put it on. Robbie stepped back, looked at Hadley and shrugged. The men never spoke. In less than five minutes the tire was changed.

The two men turned and before Hadley could offer to pay them, climbed into their wagon, nodded to Esmeralda, raised their hats to the other three women, turned their horses around on the deserted highway and with a cheery tinkling of bells, disappeared down the gravel road.

Robbie looked at Esmeralda, and in a voice mimicking the announcer on the old Lone Ranger radio show said, "Who were those overalled men?"

Esmeralda smiled, a coy, playful look shining through her dark eyes. "For now, they are zee heroes. Weeth beautiful horses."

"I'll drive," Hadley said, hurrying toward the driver's side door.

"You can't drive at night," Robbie said, a little edge in her voice.

"Oh. Right. It is going to be night soon," Hadley nodded. "But in the daytime I'm going to be like the old man who said, 'I can hardly walk, I pass out now and then, have the shakes, take twenty different pills every day, get sleepy when I'm in a car, am nearly deaf, can't see worth a damn but at least I still have my driver's license."

Mary Rose climbed into the front passenger seat. "Drive on, Robbie. Nothing confuses men more than a woman driver who does everything right."

Robbie got behind the wheel again. "Well *I'm* going to be like the young woman who got stopped and the cop said, 'I've had my eye on you for quite awhile now,' and she says 'Gee. And I thought you were stopping me for speeding." They laughed the relieved laugh of those who have been lucky and were showing it by making bad jokes.

For some reason none of them questioned, Esmeralda had never offered to drive at all.

Robbie turned on the lights and the big machine roared onto the road, the trailer rolling sedately and happily along behind it.

"Let's find a campground," Mary Rose said. "I'm pooped."

"A perfect word for you, girl," Hadley laughed. "A perfect word."

The Campground

They found it by spotting the small outline of a trailer that was the highway symbol for a campground. Robbie turned off onto the little gravel country road and moved forward slowly, the Hummer's headlights showing dense vegetation, thick bushes and a tall row of pine trees along both sides of the road. The big trailer bounced faithfully along behind.

"I bet those pines were planted back in the thirties when the WPA was putting people to work in the depression," Hadley said quietly.

"What eez theese WPA?" Esmeralda asked.

It was so dark in the car Hadley could only make out her shadow.

"Work Program Administration," Hadley replied. The government gave thousands of jobs to men who had lost so much and who couldn't find work. A lot of trees you see alongside the roads in Nebraska were planted then."

"They also went through cemeteries and recorded names on gravestones," Robbie added. "It turned out to be a terrific help to people years later who were tracking their family history."

A small, tasteful sign told them Bare Essentials RV Campground was ahead two miles.

"Two miles," Mary Rose read aloud. "And something 'optional,' but we got by before I could read it all and it was too dark."

"Probably 'full hook-up optional." Hadley said. "Or 'tent camping optional." She turned to Esmeralda. "A full hookup is what we get most of the time. It means we have sewer, electric, city water, sometimes even cable TV."

Esmeralda nodded and smiled a really twinkly smile. "I see." She said, as if there was a funny hidden meaning behind her comment.

Robbie turned into the campground. The road was lined with even thicker brush and trees. Small signs, in the style of the old Burma Shave road signs were on her right. She read them as the Hummer crept along.

"If you want
To feel just fine
Leave your clothes
Out on the line.
Bare Essentials."

"Oh good!" Mary Rose squealed. "They're environmentally conscious. They must use clotheslines instead of dryers. That's a good idea."

"Possible Humps and Bumps Ahead," Hadley read. "Watch out, Robbie, looks as if the road may get a little rough."

The road wound up a small incline and through a huge stand of oak trees.

"Park and Shed It," Mary Rose read from the passenger seat. "They must have RV storage facilities here as well." The signs were rounded and some were heart-shaped or, as Hadley thought and giggled to herself, butt shaped.

"Grin and Bare It," was the last sign before Robbie turned into the office area. Another sign told them where to park and to register inside.

"The office is closed, and it's still pretty early," Robbie remarked, climbing out from behind the steering wheel. "I'll go see if they have a night registration card." They did.

"We can pick any open site and pay in the morning," she announced, and she climbed back in and began driving the Hummer and trailer down the long, narrow road between parked RVs, many of which still had cheery lights burning inside them.

Clarabelle Southern and Bare Essentials

Mary Rose held a flashlight while Robbie hooked up their water for the night. Hadley held a flashlight and showed Esmeralda where to hook up the electricity to the trailer outlet. They didn't need the sewer for just one night, so in less than fifteen minutes they had pulled through a level site surrounded by tall, well-trimmed bushes and four big cottonwood trees. In just a few minutes, the trailer slide-outs were in place and Hadley was getting out the microwave popcorn while Robbie went through her Stephen King movies.

"How about *Misery?*" Robbie asked. "Kathy

Bates is a nurse who holds James Caan hostage in her isolated cabin. He's been in a wreck and just finished his latest novel about his heroine, *Misery*, and Kathy Bates is his number one fan."

"Is it gory?" Mary Rose asked.

"Absolutely no gore," Robbie replied. "Kathy Bates won an Oscar for it."

"I really like Kathy Bates," Mary Rose said. "I'll go to the bathroom now so I can make it through the whole movie."

"Of course she cuts the tendons in his ankles, ties him to a bed and generally tortures him," Robbie mumbled softly to herself as she slipped the disc into their machine. "But no gore."

The popcorn was starting to pop and Hadley was pouring sodas into four glasses filled with ice. It promised to be a good evening together.

Hadley was the first to wake up the next morning. She walked to the door of the trailer, opened it and stuck her head out. *I think it's going to be the warmest day we've had yet,* she thought to herself. A meadowlark was welcoming the dawn from a field somewhere close by and birds were singing in the cottonwoods surrounding them. *I bet this would be a nice place to spend a few days, just relaxing.* Her thoughts were interrupted by Robbie's head poking out the door beside hers.

"Nice," Robbie said.

Hadley nodded, "Nice." She moved toward the coffee pot and began to grind fresh beans from The Village Grinder, their favorite coffee shop.

"'Good morning!" Mary Rose said, coming up behind Robbie and giving her a quick hug. "Surprise. I liked *Misery*."

"I'm surprised, Mary Rose. "And I will say one thing, you're a good sport, girlfriend.

"You are all zee good sports," Esmeralda said. She patted Mary Rose's rear as she moved toward the table. "Hadley Joy, zee coffee smells vonderful."

They were a colorful group of early morning friends. All had on long, comfortable bathrobes. Hadley's was a thick, rich white puffed cotton. Robbie wore a blue robe with the Creighton Blue Jays logo on the shoulder and big pockets on the front. Mary Rose's robe was soft, fluffy, cozy and pink. Esmeralda, however, made Joseph's Amazing Technicolor Dreamcoat look like a shabby woman's housecoat wannabe. Her long robe had every color of the rainbow and then some. When Robbie looked at her she started to sing Andrew Lloyd Webber's song.

"And it was red, and yellow, and green, and brown." She took a breath, "scarlet, black, ocher, peach, ruby, olive, violet, fawn and a lot of colors I don't *rememmmmmmmber.*"

Hadley poured four cups of coffee and they talked about whether to eat a quick breakfast in the trailer or drive to a café in one of the small towns on down the road for an omelet. The omelet was gaining ground when Mary Rose looked out the window.

"Some other people are up early," she said. A group of three; two men and a woman, walked by on the other side of the tall hedge that ran along each side of their site.

"They look like disembodied heads," Hadley said. The hedge was so high all that could be seen of the trio were moving, bobbing heads. The woman had short grayish-brown hair, one man's head was shaved, and a shorter man's head bounced along behind them, showing only a bald spot on the very top.

They all moved to the window and they all jumped when there was a loud knock on the door behind them. A few drops from Mary Rose's coffee cup bounced out onto the couch beneath the window.

"Hello in there!" a cheery woman's voice rang out.

"It's someone to collect our fee for the overnight," Hadley said, turning toward her purse. Robbie opened the door and then began to chuckle in a friendly, mysterious way.

"Good morning!" she said. "Girls come here. We have guests."

They crowded around the trailer door, Esmeralda standing behind them. Hadley and Mary Rose put their hands over their mouths then jerked them away as fast as they could. They all smiled at the two people standing outside their door.

"Ah am Clarabelle Southern, and Ah want to invite ya'll to a cookout breakfast we have here at Bare Essentials every mornin'. We'd be honored if you'd come."

She was a large woman, one who would have not looked good being thin or small. Clarabelle Southern was sturdy, strong, substantial, and attractive and the girls looked intently at the mass of red hair on her head. They stared, too, at her warm smile, but they especially looked hard at the hair because that red hair was all Clarabelle Southern was wearing.

She pointed to her equally naked husband who had very little hair at all. "This is Bruce." Bruce took two steps toward the trailer and held out his hand. Robbie leaned toward him, shook his hand

and laughed. "Can we wear our bathrobes to breakfast?" she asked. Now they knew that Bare Essentials campground meant just that.

Clarabelle smiled a smile that made her eyes laugh. "Well Girls, here at Bare Essentials when we say, 'Clothing Optional' we mean it, Ya'll have the option to wear a sarong or go topless, or wear those nice robes. It's whatever your comfort level allows." She was nodding and smiling her welcome.

"That wasn't an 'optional hookup' on the sign, was it?" Mary Rose whispered to Hadley. Hadley smiled, and shook her head. They had stumbled into a nudist campground hidden away on beautiful Nebraska Highway 2.

Esmeralda's eyes were twinkling like never before. She leaned in between Hadley and Mary Rose and looked out the door at the Southerns. "Can you cook out zee omelet?" she asked.

There were twenty or more people gathering around a huge motor home with a spacious deck surrounding it. Some people had towels wrapped around their waists. The towel wrappers had obviously just come from the shower and were still drying off. One woman was wearing a full uniform that marked her as employed by a truck stop somewhere on the highway. She was dressed and ready to go to work. Her name tag read, "Colleen". One small, very thin older woman was wrapped in an ankle-length bathrobe which she held tight around her. Hadley noticed mittens covering her hands and she looked cold even though the morning was warm and comfortable. *The cold elderly* Hadley thought.

"This is weird," Mary Rose whispered to Robbie as they walked behind Clarabelle and Bruce. Hadley and Esmeralda were beside the Southerns engaged in what appeared to be a lively and fun conversation; They all stepped up onto the big wooden deck at the same time. A massive grill manned by an equally massive man sat to one side. Smells of bacon and sausage and hot coffee filled the air.

"There's nothin' like a cookout breakfast in a campground," Clarabelle exclaimed. "Let me introduce ya'll to our chef. This is Dickie."

"*Dickie?*" Hadley, Robbie and Mary Rose said together. Esmeralda stepped out in front of them, took the big man's hand in both of hers and said, "Dickie. Do you make zee omelet for us?"

He was naked as a Jay Bird, but in Dickie's case, it would more appropriate to say naked as a hippopotamus. Dickie was huge. Rolls of fat layered his body. His head was bald as a billiard ball, his hands as meaty as a pork roast. And he was obviously melting, fat and all, over the gypsy whose hands were holding his.

"Oh yes, ma'm, I do, I do," he said, putting his

free hand over hers and shaking it vigorously. "I
do. I do."

"He does, he does," Robbie whispered. Mary
Rose hit Robbie on the shoulder. "Stop that!" she
grinned. She leaned close to Robbie and
whispered, "I think Dickie needs a string
attached to help him find his other Dickie-do."

Robbie faked a shocked look." Mary Rose
McGill!" Hadley looked at them and laughed.

The big cook was still holding Esmeralda's
hands. He led her to a seat on a bench built into
the deck. The others followed. They sat. Six
small tables for four were on the deck. Six big
picnic tables were on the manicured lawn just
below it.

The smell of breakfast meat was delicious. "You
know," Dickie said with a delightful smile that
lit up his whole face. "You ladies aren't fully

clothing-optional yet. I realize you may be offended a bit by a naked cook.

Dickie opened the door to his motor home, grabbed something from inside and turned toward them again. He was calmly putting on a shirt.

"A shirt wasn't quite what I was hoping for," Hadley said softly. It was then that big Dickie turned his back to them and bent over a cooler filled with ice and juice sitting beside the grill. His magnificent butt looked like a smiley face turned sideways.

"I like heem, very much," Esmeralda said. "He reminds me of my gypsy men. Beeg. Strong. Powerful."

"Naked," Hadley added.

Breakfast was extremely good. Everyone gathered on the deck or at the picnic tables came to meet them. Most of those enjoying Dickie's omelets, scrambled eggs, biscuits and gravy and all the bacon and sausage you could eat were retired folks settled into Bare Essentials for the summer. Many were from Florida, come north to escape the heat.

Hadley sat beside Clarabelle at one of the small tables on the deck. Her host pointed to four people laughing together at another table. "There are Gary and Louise; Mark and Connie," Clarabelle explained. "Gary's a retired M.D., Louise was librarian for a hospice in Colorado, Mark was head of a psychology department in one of the Omaha universities and Connie was a therapist and now she's one of those 'life coaches.' If you have heart or head trouble, you go sit over there." She laughed a soft, musical laugh. Hadley liked her.

Clarabelle pointed to a couple sitting at one of the picnic tables some distance away. They were one of the few who had not greeted the girls as they came to the deck and they were obviously having a lively and perhaps even heated discussion. "That's JoAnn and Dennis," Clarabelle shook her head. "She's a former county treasurer – Democrat. He's head of the county Republicans and past master of an Elks Lodge. Once in a great while they agree with each other; then we know they're both wrong."

An attractive lady, with redder hair than Clarabelle's, approached with a carafe of orange juice in one hand and a coffee pot in the other. She wore a Green Bay Packers apron. "GiGi, this is Hadley. Hadley, GiGi." They smiled.

"Now just leavin', the one in the uniform and kissing the gentleman goodbye there, is Colleen. Makes extra fun money with a few hours at a truck stop aways down the road. Fine singer. Her husband's Walt. We call him 'Doc'. Taught math in high school. Nice. Heady and drowl, but nice and kinda cute, too."

"Oh!" Clarabelle hopped up, her whole body bouncing a bit. "Nancy! David! Come meet our guests from the city." A couple who could nearly be a mirror image of Clarabelle and Bruce came to shake hands. "They used to own an RV dealership south of Omaha. They just retired into the good life." She patted Hadley's hand. "Ya'll know, if it's a male or a machine, it's gonna give you grief. Nancy and David can fix either"

Clarabelle looked around the crowd for anyone not introduced yet. She found an older woman, deep in conversation with another lady who must have been over 80. "And last but not least, there's Lucy. The one with the notebook and pen." Clarabelle smiled a tender, loving smile. "I want to grow up just like her," she said. Then she broke into a big smile. "But I want to stay tall.

Lucy is our unofficial activities director. If there's a good cause comes by, Lucy grabs it by the tail. If there's something to be learned, Lucy sees that we all learn it. She's a wonder woman on wheels."

"You're wonderful people," Hadley said. "And I'm curious. Why clothing optional? Why be a nudist?"

Clarabelle smiled and took a sip of her coffee. "Comfort for me. Ah like the feel of the air 'gainst my skin, not cloth. And who doesn't want to be free of those bras? I tell ya. We think the human body is beautiful." She took a quick glance toward Dickie who was sitting beside Esmeralda, bobbing, nodding, smiling and listening. "Plus, there's no status here. We're all equal." She looked at Dickie again and smiled an affectionate smile. "Of course some of us are more equal than others." She laughed and patted Hadley's knee.

"Now take you girls, no offense here. Ya'll asked." She looked carefully at Hadley's white quilted bathrobe. "You're Bloomingdale's. You have the money in the group. That pretty black lady in the Creighton robe, she's into sports and probably taught. From the way she speaks, I'd say she's the smart one. And that beautiful pink bathrobe, all fuzzy and warm, and those red rimmed glasses. That lady's learned how to enjoy life and from the way gravity's worn on her, she's overcome some tough stuff."

She gazed a long time at Esmeralda. Dickie was close to a full-fledged drool now.

"And that beautiful woman in the colorful robe," her eyes glazed over as if she were headed into a mini-trance. "She is a Queen. An Empress." Clarabelle's soft southern accent was gone now. "She is a Sorceress."

Hadley was staring at Clarabelle when their hostess jumped, as if jerking suddenly in a deep sleep. "Mah word! Where did *that* come from?" She shook her head and looked distressed.

Hadley leaned back in her chair and changed the subject. "We call ourselves, 'The BOOB Girls,'" she confided. "The Burned Out Old Broads. They're my family and my best friends."

"Ain't that the 'git it all!" Clarabelle said, smiling. "The BOOB Girls. Ah like it. Ah do!"

"You know what," Mary Rose said as they walked back to their trailer. "I'm going to try it." They looked at her. The trailer was just in front of them. Mary Rose took off her bathrobe, threw it over one arm and walked, naked, as fast as she could toward their door.

"SHIT!" She said, hurrying on. Hadley, Robbie and Esmeralda straightened their shoulders, held their heads high, eyes straight ahead, tummies tucked in. Robes were thrown over arms and for a good ten seconds the four girls were totally clothing-optional, with outstanding posture.

It was nearly eleven o'clock when they drove out of Bare Essentials. The sun was high in the sky, birds were thick in the big trees and a gentle breeze was playing in the bushes. Hadley, Robbie and Esmeralda waved to the Southerns as they left the campground. Clarabelle was sweeping the sidewalk in front of the office and Bruce was tinkering with a golf cart. Mary Rose was intent on updating her PoopLog and didn't even notice them. She wasn't car sick at all.

Highway 2 stretched before them. Huge pine trees dwarfed the trees that grew far ahead in the Rocky Mountains. Fat cattle looked like black dots in amber fields. Hay bales the size of small houses sat like monarchs of the plains.

"So –," Hadley began. "If *you* owned a nudist RV park, what would you call it?"

There was a moment of heavy-thinking silence. Then Robbie spoke up." Constitution RV Resort, the resort that gives you freedom others can't." She paused for just a second. "Or – how about 'Panhandle Woodstock?'"

"I like 'Bare Buns R Us," Mary Rose added.

"That one fits our Dickie," Esmeralda said with a smile.

Then the names started coming like gun shots across the hills.
"Bare Pines!"
"Godiva's" – from Esmeralda. "I always admired her. She liked zee horses."
"Nude Dudes," from Hadley was answered by,
"Game Dames," from Robbie.
"More Bounce to the Ounce," Mary Rose said,

"for all us one-breasted Amazons."

"Scenic View," Hadley added, pointing to a sign by the road that shared the same words.

"Feel the Breeze," Robbie suggested.

"Spoon and Moon," Esmeralda said. "Eet eez more romantic."

"Cool Down Resort for those experiencing hot flashes," Mary Rose said.

"The Clothes Shed – featuring original casual attire," Hadley smiled. "Which leads, of course, to 'The Come as You Were RV Resort?'"

"Theese is such fun!" Esmeralda said.

Hadley reached out and patted her arm. "See how little it takes to amuse old people?"

She broke into the first chorus of *On the Road Again*. *I can't wait to be on the road again.* Robbie hit a button on the dashboard and Willie Nelson and his band joined them in stereophonic sound that shouted through the big vehicle.

Hawks circled overhead, joining their own laughter with the occupants of the Hummer. Another coal train rattled by them and last year's tumbleweeds crossed their path as if welcoming them to the massive sandhills. Though they didn't say anything, Hadley thought how it would be fun to invite Wes Longbow to Ft. Robinson for a few days, and Mary Rose McGill thought it would be fun to tell Wiley Vondra all about Bare Essentials RV Campground. . . in person.

Part Three

Ft Rob

Fort Robinson, established in 1873 as a frontier military post as settlers came to the Northern Plains. Over time, it became a microcosm of United States military history from that date through World War II. It served as a frontier fort, a remount station for the Calvary, a K-9 training station, a German prisoner of war camp and home in WWII of the famous Buffalo Soldiers. It is the jewel of Great Plains Indian forts.

If I could be here at any time in history, I'd be one of those gorgeous saloon girls in Crawford, that cute little town that grew up by the fort.
Mary Rose McGill

Oh, I'd want to meet Iron Teeth. The Indian woman who could ride next to a buffalo and kill

it with her hatchet. Hiyaaaaaah!
Robinson Leary

*I'd be a nurse in the WACs. That Women's Army
Corp had some tough young women in it here
during World War II.*
Hadley Joy Morris-Whitfield

*I, of course, yam gypsy. I would wander by the
fort in my wagon, sell beautiful trinkets to zee
officer's ladies, then travel on.*
Esmeralda St Benedict

*I'd want to see Crazy Horse himself. He was my
hero when I was little. Hell, he's my hero now!*
Sheriff Wes Longbow

*It would be the German prisoner of war camp
and the K-9 corps that would attract me. What
would a German POW think of these high plains
and powerful winds?*
Wiley Vondra

Spirits, Steaks and Starlight

Hadley pulled the Hummer up to the curb in front of the administration building. Once a massive barracks for enlisted men, the brick and wood structure stood proud with stately pillars and a porch lined with rocking chairs. Robbie got out and hurried inside to get their campsite.

"I'm Robinson Leary," Robbie said to the uniformed lady behind the big counter in the reception area. "We have camping reservations."

The woman's name tag read, "Marge" and she smiled across the shining counter at Robbie. "Robinson Leary." She looked at Robbie's dark skin and her smile grew. "Not related to Levi Robinson, who the fort's named after, are you?" The original Camp Robinson was named after Lt. Levi Robinson, killed by an Indian war party while escorting a supply train between Ft. Laramie, to the west, and the woodcutting camp near Laramie Peak.

Robbie smiled back. "I'm afraid my ancestry came from a little further south."

"Well make what you can of it, Ms. Leary. If you have the same name, use it." Marge gave them their paperwork, assigned them a camp site near the far edge of the campground and urged them to return soon for dinner in the large, high-ceilinged restaurant next to the check-in area. The smell of baking pies drifted toward them.

"It's the best buffalo steak in the country and believe me, it's local," Marge said.

After Hadley had backed the trailer, then re-backed the trailer, then tried backing it three more times into a shaded space that looked toward the buttes and the White River, it was nearly sundown.

"Level!" Mary Rose shouted, watching the bath-room door stay steady and not swing closed.

"Parked," Hadley said, her hands on her hips, sweat showing on her forehead. She had done the back-in and was proud. Her husband would have never let her try it with him. Well, she had done it now and so what if it took more than one, or two or five tries. She had done it!

"Let's hook it up, then," Robbie said from behind the trailer, and she started pulling out the sewer hose.

"I yam zee Electric Queen," Esmeralda laughed and she pulled the big electrical cord out from its storage door.

In just a few minutes the slides were out and the interior was set up with the coffee pot in its proper place. Their framed photos graced the counters, and Robbie's Stephen King collection was stacked neatly on the little table between the two easy chairs. The trailer had a cozy, comfortable, homey feel and cast a long shadow.

The sun was dropping slowly into the buttes to the west.

"Let's walk up to the restaurant and fork a buffalo," Hadley suggested.

"And finish by forking pie," Mary Rose added.

They grabbed light jackets and headed toward the buffalo steaks.

The road to the restaurant was lined with huge trees. Barracks that had been re-built and modernized for visitors sat beside a narrow sidewalk between the trees and the road.

"It's all so authentic," Robbie remarked. "It would be fun to work here and really exciting to go back in history and see this when some of the great Indian chiefs were here, when Walter Reed was actually the doctor, when there were hundreds of horses on the parade grounds."

"You read the brochure," Hadley smiled.

"And at one time they played polo here," Robbie said. "It was called 'The Country Club of the US Army.'"

"Look," Hadley said, pointing to a small stone monument set behind one of the log buildings to their right. They walked to it. The monument rose to just around their waistlines. It was tastefully made of stones native to the area. The top was flat with a plaque announcing that on this spot, Crazy Horse, the great Oglala Chief was killed. Lying on the flat surface beside the plaque was a small bouquet of wild daisies and a white stone.

A soft breeze blew their hair. Esmeralda moved next to the monument and placed her hand on the rough stones on the top. She looked off toward the setting sun.

"Zey would not take him there," she pointed to a vacant lot on their right. "Zee doctor would not allow an Indian into his hospital." She paused. "Zey took him there." She pointed to a small log building next to the one behind the monument. A sign, easily read through the window, told them this was a reproduction of the adjutant's office and was where Crazy Horse was carried to die.

They looked through the windows of the jail where he had been taken all those years ago.

"His spirit eez strong here," Esmeralda said in a soft, respectful voice. They believed her.

Dinner was exquisite. They ordered two huge buffalo steaks and shared them along with baked potatoes, fresh veggies and apple pie topped with ice cream. The dining room atmosphere was old west with a border above painted wainscoting showing Indians and buffalo heading away from the diners. The windows were large and tall and the setting sun cast cozy shadows across the old wooden tables.

"That was the first time I've ever eaten buffalo," Mary Rose said, as they walked back through the dimming light to their campsite. "It was delicious.'

"You've led a sheltered life, girl." Hadley said. "Less fat than cattle," she added.

"They tried crossing buffalo with cattle once," Robbie added. "Trouble was, they had the better brains of the cow and the strength of the buffalo. Tough animal to corral."

There was a gentle breeze and more stars than they could begin to count - a perfect evening to sit outside and relax. They got ready for bed, put on their bathrobes and sat up reclining lawn chairs outside the trailer. They were facing the tall buttes surrounding the fort and running along the White River where rafters enjoyed the fast flowing current and the cool splash of serious water. Hadley brought out a bottle of wine along with four glasses.

"Theese is so beautiful," Esmeralda said, looking at the stars. The sky was blanketed with what looked like a million galaxies. They sat in silence, sipping their wine, comfortable together.

"Listen!" Robbie whispered. In the distance they heard the sharp yip of a coyote. In seconds it was answered by another, even closer to them. In less than a minute a chorus rang through the buttes. Yips and howls filled the night.

"Yip! Yip-yip-yip, awoooooooooo!" Robbie howled. They joined her, yipping and howling along. The coyotes ignored them and kept on singing. Then the air was broken by the haunting shriek of a big cat.

"Bobcat? Wildcat?" Hadley asked. She looked at their shadows in the darkness and chuckled. "We obviously don't know our big kitties." The sound had been eerie.

"Royalty," Esmeralda said, bowing her head in respect. "A queen of hunters ready to feed her babies."

They were quiet again, listening to the crickets and other night sounds.

"Girls," Hadley finally said softly. "Would you mind if I invited Wes for a few days?"

"Of course not." Robbie said. She reached over and patted Hadley's arm. The lawn chair tipped on the uneven ground. Hadley grabbed the chair arm and pushed her back upright, laughing.

"Oops!" Robbie laughed. "I'd love to see the Sheriff and he would love it here, in this place."

"Speaking of which," Mary Rose said somewhat shyly. "I'd love to have Wiley come, too."

"You go, girls!" Robbie said. Esmeralda smiled and nodded.

Both Hadley and Mary Rose got up, struggling a little with their lawn chairs. "These are so low to the ground!" Mary Rose said.

"We are so old and stiff!" Hadley added. They went inside for their cell phones.

"I don't have anyone to call," Robbie said. "And that's okay."

Esmeralda reached over and took Robbie's hand. Her reclining lawn chair didn't tip at all.

"You weel Robinson. You weel." She clasped Robbie's hand and closed her eyes. "I can see heem. He eez tall and so beeg – but not beeg like our naked Dickie. Oh no. He is muscle and strong." She concentrated. Robbie looked at the outline of her face showing in the lights Hadley and Mary Rose had turned on inside. "I cannot see his name. No. I see his initials, though." She smiled. "Does N.F.L. mean anything? Do you know a man weeth these letters?"

Robbie smiled, "It stands for National Football League. I'd take an old retired linebacker with bad knees." She thought for a second. "Maybe I'd even go younger. Warren Sapp, beware!"

Hadley and Mary Rose came back out of the trailer. "They're coming." Hadley said. "Our boys are on their way."

Esmeralda did not sleep in the trailer that night.

She explained once again that she was gypsy and to sleep under the stars was where she belonged and wanted to be. Outfitted with a pillow, wrapped in a warm blanket, her lawn chair reclined to a flat cot and with the stars bright above her; she waited until long after the lights in the trailer had all gone out. Then she rose, wrapped the blanket around her shoulders and walked silently toward the raging White River and the sound of the big cat, who screamed once more into the night.

Tourism is Alive and Well in Nebraska

It was going to be a good day. Robbie left Stephen King to fend for himself and poured over brochures, went on the internet and came up with a day of fun, excitement and education, all of which were agreeable to everyone. Wes and Wiley would not arrive until later, so this would definitely be "girl time."

"We'll have the breakfast buffet to begin with," Robbie announced. "Biscuits and gravy, chicken-fried steak, eggs, pancakes, you name it. Then we all said we really want to go on the jeep ride into the buttes." They were getting dressed in jeans, long-sleeved shirts and piling up hats and sun glasses on the table to grab as they walked out. She looked around. "Where's Mary Rose? "

"Early morning phone call," Hadley said, pointing out the window to the solitary figure sitting at the picnic table. "Never a good sign, I'm afraid."

Robbie looked worried, then she shrugged. "Anyway," she went on. "I definitely want to go to the Trailside Museum after the jeep ride and see the 'Clash of the Titan.' Two testosterone-crazed mammoths fought for mating rights, got their horns locked and died. They became fossilized and are on display here, near where they were found."

"Zee males can be so foolish," Esmeralda said, shaking her head.

Mary Rose came in through the door, slowly, her head down. "I don't feel like going anywhere," she whined. "Mary Claire's divorce is getting ugly. She was crying and asking my advice – which she never did before she married, of course – and who am I to give divorce advice? I stuck it out and suffered." She was clutching her cell phone like a lifeline.

"You have to look at who owns the problem, Mary Rose," Hadley said. "I've advised and consented through four of my son's divorces, and *you do not have the answers and it's NOT your problem."* Hadley was shaking her finger as if she were scolding her friend.

"I'm sorry," she said suddenly. "I've just been there, done that, have the tee shirt. But remember the old saying, 'Didn't cause it. Can't control it. Can't change it. All you can do is listen, support her and the children and not let it get to you."

Hadley waited a second. "Actually there are options. I had a friend, a nice, calm and highly respected lady. She went into the pharmacy, walked up to the pharmacist, looked straight into his eyes and said, 'I'd like to buy some cyanide.' The pharmacist asked, 'Why in the world do you need cyanide?' My friend said, 'I need it to poison my husband.' The pharmacist's eyes got big and he said really loud, 'Lord have mercy! I can't give you cyanide to kill your husband, that's against the law! I'll lose my license! They'll throw both of us in jail! All kinds of bad things will happen. Absolutely not! You CANNOT have any cyanide.' My friend reached into her purse and pulled out a picture of her husband in bed with the pharmacist's wife. The pharmacist looked at the picture and said, 'Oh. Well. You didn't tell me you had a prescription.'

No one laughed. Robbie looked at Hadley and gave her an eye roll.

"Worth a try," Hadley said, and she plopped down in one of the easy chairs. "After all, humor helps the APEs."

"Apes?" Mary Rose looked at her and frowned.

"Anxiety Producing Experiences. We all have them, it's how we deal with them that counts."

Mary Rose plopped down equally hard on the couch, her cell phone still in her hand. "It just worries me," she said, a whine still in her voice.

"Mary Rose," Robbie sat down beside her. "Worry never changes tomorrow; it just takes away the peace of today. Worry and guilt are unproductive activities."

Mary Rose shook her head, close to tears. All at once her cell phone buzzed and vibrated. She jumped and before she could answer it, the gypsy grabbed the phone and held it to her ear.

"Allo." Esmeralda listened. "Yes. . . Yes . . .Of course. . . .Thank you." She started to hand it back to Mary Rose then pulled it to her ear again as if she'd just heard another word from the phone, "Oh yes . . . she weel like that."

They looked at her and waited, eyes wide.

Esmeralda looked squarely at Mary Rose. "That was God," she said. "God said to say to you, 'Good Morning, Mary Rose McGill. I yam handling all your problems today. I do not need your help. You go on zee jeep ride and have a miraculous day. Then right at zee end God said, 'Finish weeth some ice cream.'"

Mary Rose's eyebrows had a quick conversation with her hairline, then she jumped up. "Works for me!" she shouted. "Nobody interferes with my jeep ride and ice cream." They grabbed their hats and sunglasses and hurried out the door after her.

"How did you do that?" Robbie whispered to Esmeralda as they started up the road toward the administration building and a hot breakfast.

"Do what, Robinson?"

"You know, girlfriend. Make the phone vibrate like that."

"Zee phone always vibrates when we get a call from God," the gypsy said, and she reached over, grabbed Robbie's shoulders and gave her a quick and powerful hug.

Jeepers Creepers

"This jeep ride is R-rated," Robbie said loudly, bouncing up out of her seat as the old, customized jeep hit yet another bump on the narrow road to the top of the butte. She pointed at Hadley, "Rough."

Hadley thought for a second then caught on. "Rocky." She turned toward Mary Rose.

"Rigorous and root-filled," Mary Rose said, hanging onto her seat. She looked at Esmeralda.

"Rutted," the gypsy laughed as she bounced up from her seat as the jeep took a deep dip in the trail.

"Can you get a purple heart for riding in a jeep?" Robbie yelled at Matt, their young driver.

"Only if you jump out and find a foxhole," Matt yelled back. "Remember ladies, every brush scratch and trail dent is a beauty mark on this sucker. Oh, and **duck right now!"**

They ducked right now and a massive branch of a cottonwood tree passed over their heads.

"It's an FSJ," Matt turned sideways toward the

girls in the back and nearly hit a boulder in the process. "Full Sized Jeep." He was grinning.

"Or Future Serious Junk," Robbie yelled back. She gave him a friendly punch in the shoulder and they bounced along vigorously.

At the top of the butte they looked out over the White River valley. They got out of the jeep and climbed an even narrower trail to the very top, grabbing ahold of branches to pull themselves up and leaning into the steep climb. Matt got to the top first and held out his hand to Robbie who was leading the way for the girls.

"Come look over here," Matt said, pointing over the sharp drop-off at the top of the cliff.

They got on their knees, leaned over the edge and looked down into a huge eagle's nest below them. Inside was a young fledging enjoying a rabbit for lunch.

Matt pointed downward toward the valley. "There's where the Cheyenne ran during the Cheyenne Outbreak of 1876. They tried to follow the river north to Red Cloud and his band at the Red Cloud agency. Most of them were shot or died on the way."

Robbie nodded. "It was in January. Freezing. Horrible." She hugged herself as if she were cold. I'm interested in this. Very interested." She looked out, following the riverbed with her eyes until it vanished behind the hills.

They climbed back in and the jeep bounced and bucked its way down a different trail, through the scarred landscape of an old forest fire where thousands of new trees, planted by scouts and other groups were struggling to grow. They stopped for a few minutes to watch a buffalo herd grazing in a sunny pasture and laughed when a flock of wild turkeys strutted and hurried across the road in front of them. Sagebrush grew along the road. Matt told them it was, "cowboy toilet paper."

As suggested by God, the trip ended with ice cream.

The Museum

Wes and Wiley would arrive late that afternoon, bringing Wes' grill, steaks of the bovine variety, and - the girls had no doubt – a cooler of beer. It was Mary Rose who suggested they go back to the trailer and take naps or read until the guys arrived. It was Robbie who suggested they stop at the museum first.

The fort museum was located in a fine old house that served as the headquarters building in 1905. Holly, an attractive young woman, welcomed them.

"I'm really interested in the Cheyenne Outbreak," Robbie told her.

"We have some stuff here," Holly told them. "But the best display is in the barracks that reproduces where the Cheyenne were held and where they actually broke out into the night."

Hadley spoke up, "What do you have on the WACs of Worth War II?"

"And," Mary Rose said softly, "what do you have on the brothels in Crawford? Wasn't that the fort town in Indian days?" They looked at her.

"Mary Rose?" Hadley said, raising her eyebrows and grinning.

"She eez a woman of history," Esmeralda smiled at Mary Rose. "Or her-story. I yam sure these women of the plains were so strong and brave, especially those who survived in zee houses of ill repute.

Holly laughed. "You want a book we have here. 'Hog Ranches of Wyoming.'"

"I'm not interested in agriculture." Mary Rose looked surprised.

"Believe me, Ma'm. It's not about agriculture." Holly laughed and led them up the stairs made of rich, dark wood. When they left the museum, two full hours later, Mary Rose was carefully carrying a copy of "Hog Ranches of Wyoming."

"SHIT," Hadley said when she saw their shadows on the road as they walked back to the trailer and Hummer. And they all straightened their Shoulders, Heads went up, Eyes (I) were straight ahead and Tummy's tucked in. Their good posture lasted about ten minutes, then they got tired.

"I may read about the Hog Ranches before I nap," Mary Rose announced. But as they arrived at the trailer, Wes Longbow's Suburban pulled up beside them. Half an hour later, Wiley Vondra's old truck rattled onto their site.

Hail, Hail, the Gang's All Here

It was a quiet, relaxing evening enhanced by the energy that surrounds good friends talking and laughing together. Wes had indeed brought steaks, a quick drive into Crawford by Wiley and Mary Rose provided potatoes to bake and all the makings for a good salad. Esmeralda sent a list with them and created what she called Romani Sarma, or gypsy cabbage rolls. Hadley spread a plastic checkered cloth over the picnic table and just before they sat down, Robbie appeared with a bouquet of wild flowers she had found along the old railroad tracks near them. The wine was poured. The dinner set. The family was gathered.

"A toast to the cooks," Wiley said. And they dug in, Hadley, Robbie and Mary Rose laughing about having to go home to rest up and diet big time after this trip. Esmeralda smiled and sipped her wine. Ladybug, Wiley's doxie was sniffing out tiny pieces of steak dropped on purpose just for her.

"This is my country," Wes said as they settled in after dinner. "Land of the Lakotas, Sitting Bull, Crazy Horse, Dull Knife, Little Wolf, Two Kettles; the great chiefs."

"And Iron Teeth and all the powerful women," Robbie added.

Night had crept up the valley. The first yip came from a coyote in the hills and a full moon drifted into view. Their lawn chairs were reclined comfortably in a circle where they could all see each other. Bug lay cuddled on Mary Rose's lap, getting her tummy rubbed in gentle, long strokes.

"Full Sturgeon moon," Wiley said, looking into the sky and tossing Wes another beer from the cooler by his chair.

The big Indian popped the can open. "That's the name from the water tribes. We called it the Full Thunder Moon."

"Esmeralda's been sleeping outside under the moon and stars," Mary Rose told them.

"I yam gypsy," Esmeralda smiled.

"I yam Indian," Wes said. "I can join you."

Hadley gave him a slap on the arm. "No way, chief! You're sleeping with *me.*"

By ten o'clock they were tired. Mary Rose's cheeks were actually sore from laughing and telling the boys about Bare Essentials RV Resort. The conversation had escalated into jokes and comments to a point where she had said, "If my daughters heard me, they'd be shocked."

After Wiley said, "I heard a hole was discovered in the nudist camp wall. The police are looking into it," she grabbed the arm of Wiley's chair and, still laughing, pulled herself up. "I have to pee!" she announced, and hurried as fast as she could into the trailer.

"I forgot to ask her how her PoopLog was coming along," Wiley muttered.

The boys had comfortable rooms in the big administration building. Wes pulled out his flashlight, and taking Hadley by the hand, started walking slowly toward the road leading to the main building. As soon as Mary Rose came back outside, Wiley bowed, tipped his old Stetson and offered her his hand. The four of them walked together down the wide road, Wiley carrying blind little Ladybug in his arms.

"I'm going to bed with Stephen King," Robbie said. She walked over to where Esmeralda had gathered her pillow and blanket, leaned down and kissed her head. "Top that one, Gypsy Girl."

In just a few minutes Esmeralda saw the light come on in the trailer's bedroom. Robbie and Uncle Stevie were settling in.

Far in the hills the big cat screamed. Esmeralda stood up. "It eez time," she said. And wrapping the blanket around her shoulders, she walked toward the hills. The big cat screamed again.

Dreams come from our minds. Visions come from our souls.

Esmeralda St Benedict

They settled in. The night was quiet, broken now and then by the song of a coyote and cry of a night bird. Mary Rose was spooned comfortably with a softly purring Wiley, whose purrs were in rhythm with Bug's soft snores at the foot of the bed. She was wide awake, but getting to sleep was often difficult for Mary Rose McGill and she didn't mind. She used her awake time for prayer and meditation, repeating the consoling Catholic litanies with which she had grown up.

Robbie had stacked Stephen King beside the bed, laid her glasses on the little shelf under the window, reached up and turned off the light above her head and snuggled under the covers, her hands in prayer fashion under her cheek, the little bear secure in her arms.

Hadley's back was against Wes'. Their bed was soft and she pulled her pillow around under her cheek, sighed deeply and drifted off, an old song of romance running through her head. Wes was asleep beside her, twitching every now and then.

Esmeralda St Benedict's lawn chair bed sat empty beside the trailer.

All of humanity is connected. Sometimes one death affects the entire world for generations to come.   Esmeralda St. Benedict

Wes' Dream

Over the White River, a fog rolled in. It literally rolled, turning over and over on itself. It rolled past a dock where two elderly gentlemen were loading their fishing equipment into an old pickup after a long evening of fishing and drinking along a wide stretch of the river.

"Look at that weird fog," the taller of the two said, pointing to the roiling fog bank. "That kind of fog always kicks up my arthritis." He peered over his glasses and frowned. "Never quite saw one like that. Must be that climate weirding they talk about. Don't much like it, tell you that. Makes all my ailments act up."

The shorter, stockier man watched the moving mist for a second. "Quit complaining, Harry. You'll live to be 90."

"I am 90!"

"See? What'd I tell you?"

Both of them being a little hard of hearing, they didn't notice the beating of drums, coming from inside the rolling fog bank. It sounded very much like an Indian tom-tom.

BOOM – boom-boom-boom.
BOOM – boom-boom-boom
BOOM – boom-boom-boom.

The drums kept up a steady rhythm as the fog rolled onto land where it embraced a stand of pine trees, picked up a soft tinkling and jingling sound of bells that mixed in harmony with the drums, then moved over a hill and ever so softly marched across the parade grounds of Ft. Robinson.

BOOM – boom-boom-boom.
BOOM – boom-boom-boom

Wes Longbow always slept soundly and this night was no exception; so it was a surprise to him when he suddenly found himself wide awake and unusually alert, standing on the edge of a military parade ground in the middle of the large fort in its frontier days. It was late in the day. He knew this, but for some reason he couldn't get a sense of time or even place exactly.

There was a crowd in front of him; probably two, maybe three hundred people, all looking intently at a row of log cabins across the parade grounds. One cabin must be a stockade, a jail. Wes could just make out bars on the windows. But what were all these people doing here? There were Indians all right, dressed like they used to dress over a hundred years ago. There were white women and soldiers. Looked like there were some Beaver Men and buffalo hunters as well. What the hell was this, some kind of re-enactment? Some frontier show? Look at those Victorian dresses on the women for Pete's sake.

Then there was shouting near the jail. People were yelling and moving around. And all at once Wes Longbow was running through those milling, moving people. That's right, running *through* them. He realized he was running faster than he had ever run before and he was an Indian. Indians were known for their speed.

But, Wes Longbow wasn't pushing people aside or dodging around them to make his way past the crowd. He was running *through* them as if they weren't there, as if they were spirits…passing right through their bodies and not feeling anything…nothing at all.

He was almost to the jail. It had only taken seconds to cross the lengthy grounds. There were men coming out of the log cabin. Wes could see a young soldier stumble through the door, turn and begin to vomit. His bayonet was attached to his ancient rifle. Next came another soldier - then two Indians. A larger Indian seemed to be trying to hold a younger, thinner warrior who was bleeding from a deep wound in his back or side. There was so much blood! So damned much blood, Wes couldn't see just where the wound was but it looked bad, looked like the worst he'd ever seen and as the sheriff he'd seen some bad ones. He could see a deep cut on the larger Indian's arm as well, but nothing like the wound that other boy had suffered. The younger brave, the handsome one, staggered a few steps and fell to the ground. One move forward and Wes was beside him, looking right into his dying eyes.

The young Indian stared so deeply into Wes' face that the look bored right into Longbow's soul. Now the Indian was flat on his back. Men were gathering around him. There was shouting and Wes knew they would carry the young man into the Adjutant's office a few feet away. Somehow he just *knew* it.

The Indian actually smiled at Wes. He was dying and he smiled. Then he raised one hand toward Wes. Without so much as a thought, Wes took ahold of that hand, but he couldn't feel it. He looked down. He could see his hand, grasped as if it was holding another hand, but there was no feeling. No sensation. He could see right through his own hand.

The young man smiled up at him again. "Ciye,"
he whispered. "Ciye." And his eyes closed. The
men lifted him, Wes still holding onto the hand
he couldn't feel, following them across dry grass
to the door being held open for them. Another
Indian hurried inside. "Worm," Wes heard and
he knew it was a name. He looked at the older
Worm who looked just like the young warrior
being carried so roughly into the office to die.
"His Father," Wes thought.

Then the door was closed and suddenly Wes was
on the outside. "Hah," he thought. He had run
through all those people He could run *through*
this door. He leapt onto the door, expecting to
find himself on the other side. Nothing. He tried
again. He was still on the outside.

A woman's voice was raised behind him. He
turned. The woman was dirty. Unlike the other
women straining to see what was happening,
looking so proper and so Victorian, this one was

dressed in canvas trousers, a canvas shirt and a battered, wide-brimmed hat. She had on soldier's boots and was holding an old rifle by its barrel, the butt resting on the ground like it was some sort of walking stick. Two soldiers obviously knew her and were arguing with her.

"Yeah, well like the general said, the only good Indian is a dead Indian," the first soldier said in a loud, angry voice.

"Red devils all deserve to die, I say, Jane." came from the second soldier, just a kid, Wes noticed.

"Idjit Bastards!" The woman named Jane was yelling at them now, shaking her rifle at them like a child would shake a rattle, still holding a firm grip on the barrel.

"That was Crazy Horse, you fools! Now Camp Robinson will always be the place where Crazy Horse was killed. They'll build a monument on that friggin' blood spot and you'll be long gone and long forgot and nobody will give a damn about the liks of you."

There was a loud thump.

Wes Longbow opened his eyes. He was on the floor, fallen out of bed. A blanket was wrapped around his naked body, tangled through his legs and over one shoulder. He lifted his head and rose up on his elbows, looking at the fog slipping past the bedroom window.

"Ciye," he whispered. "Ciye. My brother." And Wes Longbow, the sheriff, put his head into his hands and wept.

On the bed, Hadley raised up on one elbow.

"Wes?"

We are all connected. When one child dies, the child in all of us weeps.   Esmeralda St Benedict

Robbie's Dream

The same thick, rolling fog seemed to change directions rather than spread out over the land. It roiled and turned in on itself, blocking out the night stars and the full thunder moon. The soft beat of the tom-toms and bells seemed to come from deep inside the dark, impenetrable greyness. It enveloped pine trees and the tall shrubs that bordered the campground. It moved in gentle slowness as it surrounded one Jayco trailer with a massive Hummer parked beside it and an empty reclined lawn chair near its door.

Robinson Leary, PhD, had gone to sleep mentally writing her paper on the creativity of America's great teller of tales. She often woke up writing in her head. It was comforting and imaginative and Robbie always found it a spiritual and magical gift of her mind; so she was surprised when suddenly she was walking up the trail to the top of the buttes overlooking an ancient Indian fort. She turned and knew instinctively that it was Fort Robinson. She also knew it was January 9, 1879, and that she was going to dread what she was about to witness.

At first she only *saw* the cold. *Strange. I don't feel it, but I can see the wind blow the trees. I can see the snow on the ground. I can even sense how the night is so crisp. It's cold out here, but I'm warm.*

She looked down. There were worn, beaded moccasins on her feet. Long leather leggings covered her legs and a deerskin shirt showed long sleeves and a decorative hem that fell below her hips. A wool blanket, obviously army issue, draped her shoulders and covered her hair. *What a strange, realistic dream,* she thought. Then she heard the gunshots and the shouts and curses of the soldiers.

Robbie leaned forward over the edge of the butte in order to see better.

Now she could feel the cold wind. Now she could see the flash of the gunfire in the distance below where she was standing and she realized she wasn't wearing her glasses.

Shouts. Horses whinnying. Shots. Smoke from rifles. More shots, too many to count. A child screaming. A child hurt, wounded. *NO!* Robbie thought. *Don't kill the children! Don't kill the children!* The sounds of horror refused to be quiet. The children refused to stop screaming. Then Robbie knew she was supposed to turn around. She did so eagerly. Anything to face away from the killing, the horrible, merciless killing that wouldn't stop.

Standing just in front of a beautiful stand of pines that crept onto the edge of the butte was an Indian woman. She was dressed exactly like

Robbie except her worn blanket fell gracefully around her shoulders and didn't protect her head.

Robbie could see her black hair, strands of it breaking out of her long braids. Beside her were a young warrior and two little girls. Close behind the woman and off to one side was a man who was obviously a chief; she knew it must be Little Wolf. She knew all these were Indians who had gone through the window of the barracks. She knew they didn't call it "barracks" either. "Prison House," came into her mind, then she looked closer at the chief and in the midst of all the terror, Robinson Leary smiled. The chief was tall, had a shock of black hair over his forehead and a strong, solid face. She had seen his picture hundreds of times. *Stephen King has a cameo role as an Indian chief in my dream, just like he did when one of his books was made into a movie.*

The Indian Stephen King smiled at her, as people smile in dreams, and nodded toward the Indian woman. *She's taller than I thought she would be,* Robbie thought. *Elfin, as in "Lord of the Rings,"* and suddenly Robbie was close enough to touch her. She reached out, but her hand simply floated though Iron Teeth and the Indian woman smiled a sad, knowing smile. She spoke to Robbie but her lips didn't open and no words floated in the winter wind. What she said went directly into Robinson Leary's mind . . . or rather, into her heart.

"You are right to be curious and filled with sorrow," Iron Teeth told her. "There were nearly one hundred fifty of us there. For eleven days we had no food. For three days we had no water. My son took one daughter on his back. I took the other." Iron Teeth was speaking in a strong, sure voice and Robbie knew this was what she was to learn from this dream.

"We ran. We ran through the snow. I found a cave. My daughter and I hid there for a week, eating what little food I had hidden in my pack from weeks before. We ate snow for water. My fingers and toes were frozen. Then they found us and took us back to the Prison House.

"After awhile my other daughter, who was only six, was found and brought to me. Her brother had carried her on his back but the soldiers had horses and guns and hate in their hearts, even for the children.

My son, my oldest was twenty years old. He found a deep pit. They hid there all night. In the morning the soldiers were near. They would find them. My son covered his little sister with leaves and dirt and told her to hide there until the soldiers were gone. He told her they would kill him and for her to wait until it was safe then go find her mother. He ran from the pit. He drew the soldiers off. They shot him. He died."

Robbie was crying, but there weren't any tears. It was as if her soul was weeping instead of her eyes. Iron Teeth stood tall. Robbie knew the rest of the story.

The commander at Fort Robinson was tired of the starvation and torture. The Indians were half in number of what they had been. Many children had died, some frozen to death. Digging mass graves takes a lot of the fight out of a man, even if he doesn't have to lift a shovel himself.

She looked for what seemed a long time at Iron Teeth standing before the pines, the grown son and small daughters by her side. Chief Stephen King apparently only wanted a small cameo. He was nowhere to be seen.

Robbie reached up and slipped the blanket off her head and draped it around her shoulders. Now she was a mirror image of the woman in front of her. *She is the Old Indian Woman Mari*

Sandoz talks about in 'Cheyenne Autumn,
Robbie knew.

Iron Teeth could ride beside a buffalo and kill it
with her hatchet. She could kill a dog and eat it
when her children were starving. She had once
endured seeing an Indian woman shot, scalped
and crawling through the dirt, not yet dead. Iron
Teeth had lived to be in her mid-nineties and
they had never broken her spirit even after they
had broken her heart. She deserved to be as
famous as the great chiefs she had followed. She
had outlived them all.

Robbie put her hand over her own heart. The
wind blew through her hair and she could feel
the cold. She could feel her toes grow numb. She
looked into the deep, sorrowful eyes of the
Indian woman. *Cuwe*, Robbie whispered. *My
older sister.*

Iron Teeth looked at her and smiled. *Tanka.* She whispered: *my younger one.*

Suddenly it wasn't January 9th over one hundred and thirty years ago. Now in her dream it was a warm night with a sky full of stars and Robinson Leary was standing on a mound near the White River; a pleasant mound of grass-covered earth with pine trees around it and a large rock on one end. And Robinson Leary knew in her soul that she was standing on the mass grave of more than seventy five Cheyenne men, women and children. She was standing on sacred ground never mentioned in tour books or in the flyers that lined the shelves in the stately main building of the fort. The grave was kept secret because there were still those who wanted to desecrate it and sell the bones. "They're just Indians," she heard whispered on the wind.

Then Robinson Leary woke up and real tears were streaming down her cheeks.

Let us be mindful that when God gave us dreams, She had a sense of humor as well as a sense of sorrow.   Esmeralda St Benedict

Mary Roses' Dream

If Carl Sandburg's famous fog crept in on little cat's feet, this one crawled on a giant feline belly. It rolled, roiled, crawled, boiled and crept back toward the main building where Mary Rose McGill had finally let go of wakefulness after two trips to the bathroom and a lengthy updating of the PoopLog on her smartphone.

There were no drums echoing a steady beat as this fog moved over the parade ground. This time, accompanying the jingle and tinkle of the bells was a distant, tinny old-time honky-tonk piano that got louder as Mary Rose spooned into Wiley Vondra's bony spine and drifted deeper and deeper into a sound sleep.

She wasn't so much surprised as interested when she opened her eyes at the end of the main street of old Crawford, Nebraska, the fort town that had been growing fast and furious after the war between the states and the Iron Horse of the railroad had steamed across the plains.

Mary Rose looked around, The piano music was coming from a beautiful Victorian painted lady; those elegant houses of multi-color pastels that stood three stories high and had wrap-around porches that just invited rocking chairs and pitchers of lemonade.

There was the rich smell of horses floating in the night air and Mary Rose turned around to see eight horses and one mule hitched to a long rail that ran across the top of a watering trough. The horses were saddled, Some were dozing, some eating from feed spread on the ground at their feet. At the end of the rail, her reins simply dropped in place, was a small, untethered spotted pony. Mary Rose smiled. The pony looked back. Mary Rose had the strong feeling that if the pony could have given her a sarcastic eye roll it would have.

She was wearing a long, plain dress of cheap cotton. It had long sleeves, an old-fashioned paisley design and she saw that simple, cheap snaps held the front closed from just below her cleavage to the hem. Cleavage! She had cleavage. In her dream both breasts were back just where they should be; maybe even a little bigger and better than in real life. Well, hey, a dream's a dream; a girl can do whatever she wants and be all that she can be, right?

Along that same line of thinking, Mary Rose's hair was piled high upon her head, like the song said. She wasn't wearing red-rimmed glasses or any glasses at all. Her boots were new and black as could be with medium high heels. As dreams go, she was looking pretty darned good.

A lively fiddle joined the piano and Mary Rose McGill opened a white-washed gate and went up the walk toward the big house. A sign before she reached the porch read, "The Singing Wren Boarding House."

The first floor of the big house contained a huge living room. Gas lights gave a soft but entirely adequate glow to the place. There was a long oak bar across one entire end of the room with numerous spittoons on the floor in front of it.

Around fifteen or twenty men sat in captain's chairs at round clawfoot tables or leaned against the bar. An intense game of poker was in progress at a table in one corner. Another had a card game going that Mary Rose didn't recognize but which seemed even more serious than poker.

What attracted her most was the big upright piano nestled between two tall windows on the wall to her left. Sitting on a clawfoot stool was a small woman with a cigarette holder in her mouth, puffing smoke as she sang some peppy song while she pounded the keys. Her hair was in spikes, a yellow Mary Rose had never seen before. She wore a bright red dress that pushed up her small breasts and she was pumping the pedals of the piano with feet clothed in equally bright red boots. She wore more bracelets than Esmeralda and huge silver dangling earrings.

A man in worn jeans with a glass of whiskey in his hand was leaning against the piano. When the tune ended he let out a whoop that made Mary Rose jump. "Why do you wear that red brassiere Dilly-O? You ain't got nothin' there to cover up."

The little woman laid her head back and cackled out a laugh. "Why do you wear *pants* Big Jack? You ain't got nothin' *there* to cover up."

She cackled again and as she started to play a slower, sadder song a midget with a fiddle made his way to a stool beside the piano, climbed up onto it and began to play along with a soft, easy melody. Mary Rose squinted, more from habit than anything else because she could see just fine. "Clyde?" she said.

Her eyes got wider. She stared at the little man. It was definitely Clyde who had eaten vanilla ice cream with them before they left.

Mary Rose walked toward the piano, sat down in a vacant chair and waited until the plaintive song had ended. There was some scattered applause and a few whoops of appreciation and the musical entertainment took a short break.

Mary Rose stood up. "Clyde?" she said again. The midget looked at her, then he looked over his shoulder to see if she was speaking to someone else. "No Clyde here, Girly-girl," he said and he pulled a flask out of the hip pocket of his old trousers and took a swig. He was wearing a shirt that looked like a red long-john top, suspenders and. . . Mary Rose glanced at his feet . . . plain, ordinary cowboy boots, obviously in a boy's size.

Her Clyde had been lifted to her bedside by the giant Rueben so he could kiss her cheek when she had her breast surgery. With or without the wedgies, sure as God loves drunks and stray cats, this was her Clyde.

She followed him to a table, sat down beside him and leaned in. "I'm Mary Rose," she smiled. "What's your name?"

"Troll." He took another pull on his flask. "You'd better get to work, Girly-girl. Momma Mary will be on your ass." He nodded toward the end of the big, shiny bar.

A woman of medium height was standing there and for the first time Mary Rose noticed there were several other women in the room, all dressed exactly like she was only with different colored dresses – all fastened with pull-away snaps down the front. Momma Mary though, was something else.

Like Mary Rose, Mary's blonde hair was piled high upon her head, held in place by colorful jeweled combs. Her earrings dangled and sparkled in the gas light, but it was her dress that caught Mary Rose's eye.

Momma Mary was wearing a Chinese komodo made of silk and bright, bright colors. It had the big draped traditional sleeves Chinese women used to actually carry tea in delicate cups as well as small dogs. Mary Rose squinted again. Even from far across the room she could see a tiny furry head peeking out from one sleeve and she had little doubt that there was indeed a tea cup in the other, just from the way the very strong and attractive looking woman was standing.

"She has a little dog!" Mary Rose said.

"Izabella, Mozzarella, Portabella Mushroom." Troll the midget said. "Izzy. She bites faster than a rattlesnake."

The piano player sauntered over and sat down. A tall glass was in her hand. She looked at Mary Rose. "Hey, Honey. You just get in?" She held out a small hand with a ring on every finger.

"Mary Rose McGill," and Mary Rose shook hands with both piano and fiddle player.

"Sweet Catholic girl," the piano player said, "Phyllis Dilly-O at your service." The woman cackled and took a long drag through her fancy cigarette holder. Her spiked hair had something on it that sparkled in the lamp light.

Two other girls dressed like Mary Rose walked by the table. One kissed Troll on top of his head then snapped open the top of her dress, leaned down and put her exposed breast against his mouth. He gave her a long kiss.

Mary Rose's eyebrows made contact with her hairline and she remembered once again the gentle kiss she had gotten from him after her surgery – on her cheek. The young woman moved on, touching her breast in a seductive way as she snapped her dress and moved toward Big Jack, still resting one arm on the piano.

Phyllis Dilly-O leaned over and nudged Mary Rose, pointing to an elderly man coming through the door, leaning heavily on a cane. "That's Horney Homer," she said. "He used to be deef as a doornail. Then the doc gave him some herb and it cured him. He could hear just fine, 'cept he didn't tell his family. They still think he cain't hear. Son of a bitch has changed his will three times already." She cackled again.

"The girls," Mary Rose said. She hesitated, not knowing quite how to ask her question.

"YOU girls," Phyllis corrected her. Then she got serious. "Ain't an easy life but it's a hell of a lot better than working a hog ranch."

"Why do they call them 'Hog Ranches?" Mary Rose asked. "Do they raise pigs?"

"You really *are* new, ain't ya?" Phyllis took a long drink. "There are pigs there all right, but they're human pigs, you could call 'em 'boars'. They're Hog Ranches 'cause the men here follow those women around like piglets follow a sow. 'Course, if they could all shoot like Calamity Jane out at three-mile, lots fewer girls would be under ground."

"They die?" Mary Rose's eyebrows did their thing with her hairline again.

Phyllis looked surprised. "Some of the girls from here are planted in the garden out back. This ain't no fancy hotel, Mary Rose. This is a mean, tough, hard life for a woman." She motioned around the room toward the other girls, some of whom were leading cowboys and solders up the big stairway to rooms on the second floor.

"The babies are buried in the rose garden," Phyllis added softly.

"Babies?"

"More of 'em die than make it," the piano player said. "They're lucky here. Momma Mary's good to her girls. They're lucky. She feeds 'em right. Gives 'em a home. Mothers 'em all. Has the doc in." Phyllis nodded to herself. "Doc's a good woman. First female doctor on the Plains. Keeps the girls clean as she can and Momma pays the whore tax regular."

"Whore tax?" Mary Rose seemed to have a lot of questions.

"Gotta pay the town, little girl. Doc comes in, town gets paid."

Phyllis was ready to play piano again. She gave Troll a kick. One of the girls had been sitting on his lap, her dress unsnapped to expose her breasts just above his eye level. He shoved her off his lap and stood up.

"I don't like you nearly as well as when you were Clyde," Mary Rose whispered to herself. Then she looked up to see Momma Mary standing over her.

"I know you're new, Sweetheart. I'm going to start you off easy." The cute little dog peeked out

of the big sleeve. Mary Rose reached up and
scratched the little ears and Izzy licked her hand.
She didn't bite at all. Being a smart dog, maybe
she only bit Troll and the men.

"Val here will treat you right and teach you
well."

Val was tall, handsome and had ridden the trail
so much that the seat of his jeans was worn
through. Standing behind him you could see his
rough, bare butt. He actually held out his hand
politely to Mary Rose. The holster at his side
was empty. Momma Mary must require guns to
be checked at the bar. *Good idea,* Mary Rose
thought.

Before Val could invite Mary Rose upstairs, a
young soldier from the fort staggered over,
obviously drunk. "Let's see what she looks like
first, Val."

He reached out, grabbed the top of Mary Rose's dress with both hands and before she could even take a step back, gave it a strong yank. The entire front of the dress flew open, letting anyone in the room who was watching see that Mary Rose McGill was totally naked beneath the thin fabric.

That's when Momma Mary pulled back her big sleeve, took a delicate tea cup from inside it, carefully set the cup on a table and gave the young drunk a knockout punch right between the eyes. His eyes crossed for just a second, then he fell backward, spread-eagled onto the floor. A huge black man Mary Rose had not noticed before walked over, picked up the soldier like a rag doll, carried him to the door and threw him outside. Phyllis started playing "When Johnny Comes Marching Home Again on the big piano. Troll and his fiddle were climbing onto the stool again.

Val turned to Mary Rose who was so startled she hadn't even pulled her dress together over her bare body. The cowboy smiled at her. "Well as long as you're all set to go . . . .," he said. He nodded toward the stairs and held out his hand.

That's when Mary Rose McGill, sweet Catholic girl, woke up. She was sitting up in bed, holding the sheet against her chin. Her eyes were wide with fear.

"What a horrible, hard life!" she said out loud. "Those poor women."

She felt her chest. There was just one breast there. "Thank God!" she said. And thinking of the babies buried in the rose garden and the women struggling to survive at the Hog Ranches, Mary Rose put her head in her hands and softly began to cry.

Some dreams teach us of things before our time. Others, more terrifying, tell us of our past. If your heart is good, those dreams can be healing.
Esmeralda St Benedict

Wiley's Dream

The fog didn't move away from the main building where Wiley and Wes had rented the airy, comfortable rooms. Instead, it began to move in on itself so quickly it looked like a grey pot of water coming to a boil; continually swirling and twisting.

There was no longer a honky-tonk piano and a lonely fiddle accompanying the jingling, tinkling bells. Now Vic Damone was crooning *My Heart Cries for You . . . dies for you, sighs for you* so softly it was like a whisper.

Wiley Vondra had never told Mary Rose McGill or anyone else what had happened to him in 1951, a year when he was coated with so much sweat it had lost all its odor and just poured clean out of his body, a year when he dressed to match the jungle and smoked two packs of cigarettes a day and his best friend was an Army-issue rifle.

But Wiley Vondra wasn't in Korea anymore and he wasn't sleeping cozy and warm beside the sweetest, most innocent woman he had ever met, either. No, Wiley Vondra was walking through the door into a small room where a husky German was seated on a cheap cot behind barred windows with a wash basin beside his bed and a small radio on the floor next to him. Bill Haley's *Rock Around the Clock* was giving out the one o'clock, two o'clock, three o'clock rock rhythm of the decade, and Wiley knew he was supposed to sit down next to the German, who was offering him a cigarette and smiling.

"I quit smoking in 1980," Wiley said. He took the cigarette, put it in his mouth and the German struck a match and lit it. Wiley sat.

"POW?" Wiley asked.

"Ya," the German said.

In 1943 the German prisoner of war camp at Fort Robinson was equipped to house 3,000 prisoners who worked the fields, tended the horses and kept the fort in order. Now Wiley Vondra was talking to one. This seemed to him a strange, eerily real dream and he knew instinctively what he was there to do.

"I never talked about this before," he said. He looked at the floor instead of his host who reached under his cot, pulled out a hidden bottle of cheap whiskey and handed it to Wiley. Wiley took a drink and handed it back.

"It was Korea," Wiley smirked, "the forgotten war. The first war we fought where we learned we didn't always win; where everybody lost."

Perry Como and Betty Hutton were being way too happy on the old radio now with *A Bushel and A Peck and a hug around the neck.* As far as Wiley was concerned, they could take their barrel and a heap and shove it in their sleep.

"It was just one day," he told the German. "You know how one day can affect your whole damn life?"

"Ya," the German smiled a knowing smile and nodded. "Ah, ya!"

Wiley looked at the big man's prison-stripe shirt. "Yeah, buddy. I guess you do, don't you."

"Well this day was hotter than hell, like usual. We were on patrol and our lieutenant seemed to know about this Gook village. At least he led us right to it, and before I knew it we were stacking brush and dried tree limbs around one little shack. Hey – so what, the place was deserted, empty, this was just a little urban renewal project. Why, when the boys burned villages in Viet Nam they just threw torches on the roofs. We had to work hard and stack brush in Korea." Wiley gave a smirky, tired laugh. The German nodded.

"So I got out my army issue cig lighter, set it to the kindling and it catches like a son of a bitch. But then . . ." Wiley took a long drag on his cigarette and leaned back against the wall behind the cot. It tasted good. "Then I heard a little kid start to scream, and this little girl came running out of *my* shack, her mother chasing her and the little kid. . . " Wiley choked. "The little kid was on fire for Christ's sake! And her mother caught her up in her arms and ran into the trees. Both of them were throwing off smoke. I just stood there. I couldn't move. All the other guys stood there too, then the shacks started burning and the lieutenant yelled for us to move out."

There was a pause and Wiley breathed a deep, sad sigh. From the tinny radio, Johnny Ray encouraged everybody to *Cry*, so Wiley did, softly, the image of a burning child burned into his brain.

"That was just the morning," he said after he had collected himself. The German reached into his pocket and pulled out a grey handkerchief. Wiley took it and blew his nose.

"The afternoon was about over and we were moving through the jungle, mosquitos thick on our backs, and we meet an enemy patrol coming our way. Long story short, we shoot; they shoot. We pushed 'em back but as we moved through where they were, we came onto this kid. Young Korean. He dropped his gun and held up his hands for us to take him prisoner." Wiley looked at the German.

"Like you, big fella."

The German smiled a sad smile, "Ya."

"Yeah. You relate to that." A deep breath.
"Yeah. Well our smart-ass lieutenant was leading
from the back. He and I were the last ones to
pass this kid. Our fancy officer says to me, 'We
aren't here to take prisoners. Shoot him,
Vondra.' And he moved on toward the other
guys.

"The kid and I are standing there, staring at each
other. Then he nods, makes a motion to let me
know he's going to reach into his pocket. When
he does he pulls out a picture, an old photo and
turns it so I can see. It's three people; a young
woman, an older woman and a baby. It's his
family. And I'm supposed to kill him." The
German nodded.

"Ya," he said again.

"Ya. Instead I motion with my head toward the

jungle and say to the kid, 'Run! Run damn it!'
The kid catches on and he runs. But instead of
running *away* from us, he runs toward where our
platoon has gone. He was so young and so scared
he got confused. I shot into the air to make the
guys think I'd shot the kid, but then …"   Wiley
blew his nose again.

"Then I heard the real shot and one of my
platoon – not the bastard lieutenant of course –
blew the kid's brains out." Wiley sighed.

"If only I'd turned him around and pushed him
in the right direction. If only I'd told him to just
stay where he was. If only I'd not lit the
kindling."

"Eff honly," the German repeated.

"Eff honly," Wiley said. "If only in the big WW
Two was called 'Shell Shock', in Korea we had
'Battle Fatigue,' now the kids have 'Post

Traumatic Stress Syndrome' and we're still fighting wars we can't win. Stupid, stupid, stupid."

Wiley sighed, leaned back. The German was leaning back against the wall beside him. The music had changed again. Now Les Brown and his Band of Renown was taking a *Sentimental Journey home.*

"I came back. Used the GI Bill to get a degree in agriculture at Iowa State then moved back to my folk's farm outside of Louisville." He looked at the German. "That's just outside of Omaha . . . east of here aways" The German nodded again. Wiley went on. "Ran some Angus cattle. Farmed with my dad. Expanded the farm, never talked about his war or mine. Knew some good women. Never married any of 'em." Long pause. *Sentimental Journey* was ending; so soft, so sweet.

Wiley looked at the German prisoner of war. The German looked back. Connie Francis began to sing, *Who's Sorry Now . . .who's sorry now.*

Wiley Vondra smiled a sad smile. "Me," he said. "I'm still sorry."

Wiley was lying flat on his back when he woke up, safe and snug in the big bed, Mary Rose warm and still beside him, also on her back.

"Mary Rose? You awake?"

"Yes. I had a kind of bad dream and I've been watching that strange fog. Look at it, Wiley. It moves and sometimes I hear bells." Wiley turned his head and they stared out the big window into the heavy, moving greyness.

Wiley laid his head on Mary Rose's chest - on the side where her breast had been.

"There's something I want to talk about," he said. "I've never told you my story and why I cry sometimes in the shower."

Mary Rose reached up and smoothed his forehead. "You're a good man, Wiley Vondra." She moved her head, kissed him gently then snuggled down to listen. Ladybug crawled up from her spot at the foot of the bed and nuzzled her way under Mary Rose's arm to lay her head on Wiley's chest.

When our dreams inform us of our pasts, they tell us of our strengths. Esmeralda St Benedict

Hadley's Dream

The fog didn't move away from the fort's main building. Mary Rose had laid her head on Wiley's and was wiping his eyes with the edge of their sheet as he, for the first time, marched someone he cared about through the jungles of

Korea with blind Ladybug dozing contentedly between then. Mary Rose didn't see that the fog lightened just a shade. She didn't hear the music change from the 1950's to Glen Miller's big band softly playing *String of Pearls.*

Hadley Joy Morris-Whitfield, sound asleep just down the hall heard it, though. Hadley Joy heard it coming from a big console radio hooked up in a garage that smelled of axle grease and gasoline and metal. A hanging job light glowed from the ceiling, so bright it illuminated the whole room.

A small man's boots stuck out from under a dirty World War II jeep. He was lying on one of those crawlers Hadley's dad had kept in his garage. He had pushed Hadley on it more than once when she was six or seven years old.

She looked around. The music was loud. Glen Miller was good. She and her girlfriends had learned to jitterbug to his tunes and even now, in her dream, she found her body starting to move to the easy rhythm.

A cracked mirror hung over a long work bench and Hadley glanced up and into it. She jumped and her eyes widened. She took two steps toward it and peered in. It was her reflection, but she was young. She wore a uniform. And her hair! She reached up to feel her hair. It was in a tight roll around the back of her head at her collar line, wrapped around what her mother had called a "rat" – one of those soft mesh things women used back then. You could wrap it around like Hadley's was now or you could make a French twist and fasten it with hairpins. Yep, There was a hairpin all right. Hadley pulled it out, looked at it, smiled and stuck it back.

Her lipstick was a bright red. She smiled again. Just two colors in those days, pink and red. "Kinda cute," she thought as she took in the uniform. WAC. Women's Army Corps. One hundred and fifty thousand strong after 1941. Serving all over the world while Rosie the Riveter took care of the home front.

Hadley rather liked the way she looked. She had a waistline and her breasts were, to put it delicately, "perky."

She lifted her chin, put her hands on her hips and started stepping back to get a fuller view of herself in the mirror. On her second step she caught her foot in the crawler. She gasped, twisted around to catch her balance and her foot flew out of the crawler with a hard push. She made a futile grab for the door handle of the jeep, missed and landed hard on her butt on the concrete floor. The pushed crawler and its passenger shot out the other side of the jeep and a woman's voice said, "What the hell?"

Hadley, still on the floor, slid sideways and turned toward the angry footsteps coming around the jeep. Approaching her was a small, very young woman in Army fatigues, heavy black boots and minimum-maintenance hair. She was carrying an over-sized wrench held high. She looked like she was ready to use it on Hadley.

"And *who* the hell are you, Dingbat?" The young woman yelled out the question.

Hadley looked at her, squinted, took a second look and said, "Maggie? Maggie Patten?"

The young WAC stopped short. She peered down and frowned. "Yeah, the Maggie's right you stupid dame. But the last name's Dohe. You gotta beef about that, soldier?"

That's right, Hadley thought. *She's not married yet.*

Hadley struggled to her feet, brushing dust off her slacks and smiling. "Ranch close by, in the sandhills. Your brother is Homer." Hadley held out her hand. "Hadley Joy Morris." Hadley used her maiden name.

Maggie threw the wrench on the floor, wiped her right hand on her butt and held it out. Her face was smudged with grease and spots of grease had matted in her hair. Hadley couldn't help but smile.

"I know about you, Maggie and I also know you can't be more than fifteen years old right now. That means you lied to get into the WACs and you got stationed just a few miles from your dad's ranch because the recruiter probably went along with it. Doesn't surprise me a bit."

Maggie Dohe Patten had not just been one of the original BOOB Girls at Table 12; she had been their organizer, their inspiration, their soul sister. Maggie Patten, when Hadley knew her outside this strange dream, had been old, saucy, bossy and bold. It was Maggie Patten who convinced them they could run away and leave no forwarding address. It was Maggie Patten who got them the Hummer and trailer from her brother's ranch, was friend to a giant bull snake named Methuselah and who had fired five shots into her dead husband's tombstone and loved every minute of it.

The three other friends, Hadley, Robbie and Mary Rose had fastened Maggie's suitcase around her dead body, put a plastic-wrapped photo of her missing son in her jacket pocket and buried her at sea. Totally illegally. Maggie had died suddenly on a cruise they had toughly enjoyed and during a raging storm they had thrown her overboard. It was what she had wanted.

Hadley smiled. She had a strong memory of them struggling to get Maggie's body over the railing. She was small, not heavy, but they were old and had never been candidates for women's weight-lifting competition. The body and suitcase had landed on the railing below them, balanced there precariously, then to their great relief, slid into the angry waves beating against the ship.

Now here was young Maggie and Hadley's grin went from ear to ear. She moved forward, without thinking, to hug the young woman, but Maggie took a quick step back, nearly bumping into a handsome young soldier coming through the open door just as the entire Glenn Miller band yelled, "PENNSYLVANIA SIX FIVE OH-OH-OH!"

"Whoa, Dohe," the young man said. He stepped past Maggie and walked toward Hadley. He was tall, blond, dressed in fatigues identical to those Maggie wore and his name tag read, "Marvin."

"And who are you, Beautiful?"

He moved quickly and close to Hadley. He smelled of cigarettes but not in a bad way and his voice was like brown honey.

He smiled and laid a hand on Hadley's rear. That was not in a bad way either. He leaned in and whispered in her ear.

"Give me ten bucks and I'll do anything you want, Baby."

Hadley leaned close, let her breasts brush his chest and whispered back, "Good. Here's ten bucks. Clean my apartment."

The young man slapped her butt and laughed.

The young Maggie growled at him. "She's a new skirt, Stu. Keep your hands off."

Hadley had started to enjoy this dream. She wasn't sure she wanted Stu to keep his hands off.

She winked at him and then jumped when a door slammed open behind her.

"Stu! You two worthless women! Follow me, dammit, I need help."

A svelte woman in a nurses' uniform was halfway into the garage, looking anxious and in control at the same time. Her hair was coal black and a large dark birthmark across one entire cheek was somehow strangely attractive and seductive.

"Whazup, Janice?" Stu asked, starting to move toward her.

"Got a grunt here with a bullet through his ass, a broken knee and no doc. I need you to hold him down while I dig the slug out."

"Where are the medics?" Maggie asked as they started hurrying after Janice.

"They took off for Crawford and some rocky mountain oysters," Janice explained. "All my nurses are at Chadron State getting some new certification. This always happens when you figure you'll have a quiet day."

They were trotting behind Janice, shooting around another building, through a small yard and into what was obviously the base hospital. Janice banged through a door that had "Kilroy was here" scrawled on it and in a second they were inside. Another soldier, who looked to be in his mid thirties, was lying face down on an old fashioned army bed, except for this era, there was nothing old fashioned about it. His backside was bare as the day he was born and covered with blood.

"Do we need to wash our hands?" Hadley asked.

Janice frowned at her. "I just want you to hold him down, not pet him."

"Sometimes I faint," Hadley said. They looked at her.

"Not this time!" Nurse Janice barked at her.

"Jesus," Maggie said. "What'd our dumb-ass quartermaster do to himself?"

Janice snorted. "Like a moron he was up on the butte showing off, shooting wild turkeys." She snorted again. "I should say shooting *at* them. Can't hit the side of a barn. He slipped, fell down the butte, smashed his knee and managed to shoot himself in his ass at the same time. Not everybody can do that."

Hadley moved to the soldiers head. "Hi," she said softly. He raised his head to look at her. He had sandy hair, a strong face streaked with tears, and a scar across his chin. He looked pitiful and scared and humiliated.

She looked at him. Then she looked at him
again. She squinted just as she had when she first
saw the young Maggie Patten in the garage just
minutes before. There was a few seconds of
complete silence.

"Dad?"

He looked back at her, acting like he was ready
to start bawling. He gave her a "you look kind of
familiar" stare for a second then buried his head
in his pillow.

Hadley's mouth hung open. This was her father.
She would be a little girl right now, back home
with her mother, helping her hang a star in their
living room window to show they had a soldier
overseas. But Fort Robinson, Nebraska, was
definitely *not* overseas.

"Hey!" Janice yelled at her. "Help hold the old
bastard down, dammit!"

Maggie's body was spread across the man's middle. Stu Marvin had his legs in a killer grip.

Hadley looked at them. Whatever young Maggie saw in her face softened her. She gave Hadley a soft smile and said, "Don't pay Janice no mind, Kid. She's steppin' out with an undertaker from Maine. He just shipped out."

Hadley looked at Janice pushing a tray of instruments toward the bed. She looked at Maggie looking back at her, smiling that smile she had loved and lost. Then she was sitting up in bed, tears dampening her cheeks, looking at Wes who was standing at the window, a blanket wrapped around him, looking for all the world like an old-time Indian chief without the war bonnet. The fog outside was vanishing into white, wispy ribbons. The jingling, tinkling bells were silent.

Without turning toward her Wes said,
"Interesting dream?"

"My dad. . ." Hadley began. "He told everyone
he was hurt parachuting into enemy lines in
World War II. He told everyone that was what
smashed his knee. He told everyone he was a
hero and he'd given his purple heart to an orphan
boy overseas to sell for food. The VFW adored
him. He rode in parades. My mother told me he
was on a secret mission and his letters were sent
somewhere in Nebraska to be postmarked so no
one would know where he was." She stopped
and took a breath.

"But he was right here," Wes finished for her. He
moved to the bed and sat down beside her.

"He so wanted to be a hero, but he was just an
older soldier who had enlisted and was sent here
to take care of food and supplies. It was all a lie.
We could have come here and lived with him.

Did my mother know? She had to suspect something." Hadley was twisting the sheet and looking distressed. Wes put his arms around her.

"Does it matter?"

She was quiet for a minute. "Not in how I love him," she whispered. "But he didn't have to make up a secret life. He was my daddy, my hero. I never knew he was so insecure and so afraid." She laid her head on Wes' shoulder and he laid his head on top of hers.

Riding the Long Freight Home or in this Case, A Wagon

They had agreed to meet for breakfast at nine, but they were all awake when a tree full of fat, blackbirds crowed in the dawn. Wes walked across the old parade ground toward the monument to Crazy Horse. Robbie was standing in front of it holding a bouquet of wild daisies and greenery picked from the side of the road.

Wes walked up beside her and laid a cigarette and a white stone on the monument.

"You don't smoke," Robbie said.

"I still carry. And he loved tobacco."

"They spelled his tribe differently than usual on the plaque," Robbie said softly, her fingers tracing the letters. "I usually see the tribe spelled 'Oglala', but here it's spelled like the town. 'Ogallala.'" She looked up at Wes. "Should have spelled it right."

Wes nodded toward the flowers in Robbie's arms.

"For Iron Teeth. She doesn't have a monument, but she should." She nodded toward the barracks that told the history of the Cheyenne Outbreak and where Robbie had first seen Iron Teeth's picture. She walked over and laid the bouquet on the ground in front of the door. A soft breeze brushed her hair.

"I doubt she was much for flowers. But I'm much for breakfast. I think we all had a rather busy night." She walked back to Wes, took his hand and they began to walk toward the main building and the rich, welcome smell of cooking bacon and sausage.

Wiley was finishing his shower. Mary Rose was making an entry in her PoopLog and playing with her smart phone.

"Wiley," she said loudly. "The news on my phone says a study shows women use 30,000 words a day compared to men's 15,000." She chuckle. "I think that's because women have to repeat things to men all the time."

Wiley stuck his head out of the bathroom. "Did you say something, Mary Rose?"

Hadley was first to reach the restaurant. She ignored the two young women behind the big counter, paid no attention to the delicious smells emanating from the kitchen and hurried instead to the stairs leading up to the second floor. As fast as she could she climbed the stairs, breathing hard as she reached the top. The top floor, used for meetings and a glorious Christmas dinner for sandhills residents for miles around, was empty. But the walls were hung with photos from World War II.

"Thank God for Robbie and her brochures or I wouldn't have known about this," Hadley said aloud to the empty room. She moved around the hall, glancing quickly at the pictures. Nothing. No familiar face. No Quartermaster. No WWII fading into history.

She circled one end of the room, walked along one wall. Then she saw him. There he was. Standing with his arms around two other GI's in front of the building with the Quartermaster sign on it. She smiled, reached up and touched his face. "Oh Daddy," she said softly. "You didn't have to pretend. You didn't have to lie."

Later that day she would show Wes and everyone else. Later that day she would take Robbie and Mary Rose to the WAC section of the fort museum and see if they could find a picture of their young Maggie. Later that day.

Esmeralda was sitting at a big corner table when Hadley came downstairs. Wiley and Mary Rose were walking up the steps to the historic old front doors. Ladybug had been lovingly placed on her pillow in Wiley's truck where she loved to sleep.

Hadley glanced out the window behind Esmeralda and smiled when she saw Robbie and Wes coming across the parade grounds holding hands. *We've all had an interesting night*, she thought to herself, and she walked across the dining room and sat down beside a gypsy who looked surprisingly refreshed.

"I yam famished!" Esmeralda said before they could all sit down. She led them to the buffet and they watched as she piled on scrambled eggs, six strips of bacon, four link sausages and a stack of biscuits. When she smothered her biscuits with sausage gravy a little dripped from her plate back into the heated tray. "Ah," she smiled and she took a deep breath of good cooking.

The rest of them had filled plates, but the rest of them looked somewhat tired.

Esmeralda began to eat, saying nothing.

"OK," Hadley said at last. "We all had dreams, right? Who goes first?"

Wiley took a deep breath. "I will," he said. "I need to be able to tell it without breaking down."

Esmeralda was sitting next to him. She reached over and touched his arm. "We do not break down, my Wiley. We break out into new freedom. Tears are cleansing." She took another bite of biscuit and gravy, chewed, then said, "But you will not cry this time."

He didn't. He told the whole story of Korea. They listened, eyes wide. Only Mary Rose and Esmeralda kept eating. When he was through he sighed, smiled shyly and pointed his fork at Wes Longbow.

"You're next big Injun."

"I saw Crazy Horse die," Wes began.

They stared at him.

"Eat." Esmeralda said to them. "Theese food eez too good to become cold." She was eating as if she would never eat again.

Wes told about flying through the crowd, seeing the woman he was sure was Calamity Jane herself, of holding the hand of a legend.

Mary Rose described Phyllis Dilly-O and the very different Clyde the Troll. They laughed at her description and cringed when she told of nearly being dragged upstairs as a boarding house lady of the evening.

Robbie described Iron Teeth and the Cheyenne Outbreak in such detail that they were all leaning toward her, totally unaware of their server refilling their coffee cups then staying to listen for a few minutes.

Hadley became excited when she said she had seen a teenage Maggie and Robbie and Mary Rose broke into huge grins. She told them of her father and how he had lived a false life when he hadn't needed to.

It was a good two hours later that Esmeralda stood. She had actually scurried back to the buffet and refilled her plate once, commenting when she returned to the table that people often did not appreciate "zee vonders uff gude food." Her accent seemed to be getting heavier again and she actually seemed to be getting thinner. *Wonder how she pulls THAT off,* Hadley thought, then convinced herself she was seeing things.

But now Esmeralda was standing, looking out the window toward the campground.

"Eeet eez time to go," she said softly, a note of sad finality in her voice.

"It sure is!" Mary Rose exclaimed. I can't wait to change clothes and get to the museum to see if we can find Maggie. I want to see everything."

Esmeralda moved beside her and gave her a quick, surprising hug. "You are right, Mary Rose. It is important not to miss anything in life. But first we go to zee trailer."

"Something's up," Hadley said to Wes as they went out the door. She was very curious about what was going on with their beautiful, hearty-eating gypsy friend.

The trailer sat waiting for them. The sun was high in the sky now and a cool breeze blew down from the distant mountains to the west.

Elsewhere on the fort the jeeps were being readied for the butte tour, young people were gathering to raft down the White River, eagles soared over the high butts and the coyotes slept.

They were the only campers in the entire campground.

"Must be the slow season," Wiley commented.

The night before there had been at least six other RVs of various sizes and shapes in the big space. Now there was only the wind and their Jayco and the big Hummer being patient beside it. The Hummer looked lonely. Maybe it wanted to go home and be parked beside Frieda's pink Cadillac.

Then they heard it. The tinkling, jingling bells that had ridden the fog into their dreams. They stopped, moving close together, standing in the center of the empty campground. Esmeralda, who had been in front of them, stopped as well. She turned to them. She smiled. "I must go." The thick, roiling, moving fog was coming in behind her and with it were shadowy shapes, getting closer and closer.

They were quiet. Wes had moved between Hadley and Robbie and had an arm around each of them. Mary Rose and Wiley had their arms around each other as well.

They waited. In just a minute the shapes became horses; the same huge, beautiful black horses that had pulled the big wagon carrying the two men who had changed their tire on Highway 2 a few days ago. But this time the huge, beautiful horses were pulling a fabulous, gaudily decorated, very elaborate gypsy wagon. The seat of the wagon was empty.

The jingling bells they had all heard were on the horses' collars and tack. Bells were even attached to the ribbons that held their tails in a show position. Bells were braided into their manes. The horses pranced, shook their heads and snorted a hello to Esmeralda. Tinkling bells lined the red canvas roof of the wagon. The sounds were familiar to everyone standing there.

They looked at their friend as she reached up and petted the horse nearest her. Then she walked over and took Hadley's face in her hands. A single tear rolled down Hadley Joy's cheek.

"You have seen the strength of being who you are, of honestly, of love and you share it well, Hadley Joy." She looked from one to another of them. Their faces were serious.

"You all have strength that is amazing," she said with certainty. "You carry burdens and smile. You are willing to grow, to laugh and enjoy each other." She looked at Robbie, then Mary Rose then Hadley. "You go with a frightened friend to zee doctor's or zee hospital. You are loyal. We do not always find our family in zee place where we were born." She nodded at them. "You are zee best kind of family – the one that eez chosen."

She moved to Robbie, "Robinson. You have touched the power of women of color and all women." She smiled a sly smile, "And always remember, your Stephen King had as his hero in *The Stand* the oldest woman in America. Mother Abigail was. . . how deed he say it? A gnarled apple tree still green with lovely life? Yes. Oh give me zee older woman every day. Zee older woman eez zee wise woman, zee beautiful woman. She eez zee woman who deserves honor and glory."

She moved to Mary Rose. "And she eez zee woman who, in her aging, becomes zee butterfly. Mary Rose, you, like zee others, have touched both knowledge and wisdom in your dreams."

She laughed a small, loving laugh and touched Mary Rose's cheek. "Knowledge and wisdom As you say, 'knowledge is knowing a tomato eez a fruit. Wisdom is not putting eet in a fruit salad.'"

Esmeralda threw back her head and laughed again. Her dark hair sparkled in the sun. Her cheeks were shining. "Most of all, you all have zee wisdom to not take life too seriously. You love each other. You appreciate beauty and see yourselves as beautiful." She looked at the two men. "Even you, Wes and Wiley. You are beautiful, too."

She touched Wes' hand from where it rested on Hadley's shoulder. "You lived your heritage, Wes. You held zee hand of your history. All should do so, for our roots can give us pain or give us power, whichever we choose."

She became very serious. "Shunkaku," she put her hand on Wes' shoulder.

He looked surprised and replied softly, "Tanke."

Esmeralda merely smiled her soft smile and nodded. She had spoken in his native Lakota language. She had called him affectionately, "younger brother." He had called her his "older sister." There was a comfortable contentment on his lined face. She took a step and put her hand on Wiley's cheek. It was damp. "Oh Wiley. You have learned to share your soul. All of us have zee painful memories. All of us must be kind to all we meet for they, too, have painful memories." She smiled. "And sometimes zey are just having a bad day. So let us be kind and loving."

The horses whinnied and pranced. Esmeralda sighed and smiled a sad smile.

"I must go now. Eet has been wonderful being your BOOB Girl buddy." She looked at their questioning faces, their puzzled expressions and how they appeared to almost be in a trance. She laughed softly one last time.

"As zee old saying goes," she said. "We have

friends for a reason, a season or a lifetime. I was here for a reason. You have found yourselves to be friends for a lifetime." She paused. "I vas also here for my own enjoyment. I had a vonderful time."

She walked gracefully to the wagon. She seemed to float, as she had a year ago when she walked to table 12 at Meadow Lakes. The horses lifted their heads and shook their manes. The bells jingled and tinkled. She grabbed the handhold on the wagon, climbed onto the step and in one fluid movement of her colorful skirt, took her place on the driver's seat and lifted the reins.

Behind the wagon the fog thickened. She raised her arm in a goodbye salute. The glorious horses turned in a wide circle, their bells jingling with every step. In the distance the big cat screamed and Esmeralda St Benedict, the gypsy, drove slowly into the fog and disappeared.

The End.

Ft Robinson Photos

Iron Teeth, old Indian woman.

Crazy Horse marker,
memorializing the spot of his death.

German prisoner of war

Present-day administration building with great
buffalo steaks and where the fog met Wes, Hadley,
Wiley and Mary Rose.

A word of thanks:

A huge bookcase with lots of room to Stephen King, who is one of America's greatest tellers of tales and with whom I've spent hours – always with his book, not the king himself.

A year's supply of tasty cones to our Old Market Neighbors at Ted and Wally's who do know how to make a sundae.

A raised cup of great coffee to all the owners and manager of every wonderful restaurant in the Old Market and to Michael, Roba, Melissa and Floyd who keep our Mayfair apartment in great shape.

The website for the Lakota Words I used doesn't seem to have a name, but it comes up when you Google under "Lakota Words" and I love it. Thanks to whoever created it.

Warm summer breezes to our terrific friends at beautiful Fort Robinson. We discovered Ft Rob years ago when David Prowse, who played Darth Vader in Star Wars worked with us in programs for children with disabilities. He was from Britian and wanted to see "real Indians" so we took him to the sandhills and he loved it.

We loved, and still do, Vince and Marge Rotherham, superintendents then. Vince died awhile back but Marge helped us with the history we needed for this fun book, as did Ed Bieganski. Holly Counts at the fort museum found the Hog Ranches for us along with the 1880 census of the Crawford boarding houses. And thanks to Tom Buecker, fort historian and writer of real books on its history. It was Tom who introduced us to the fantastic Iron Teeth. Her story needs to be told and you can read about it by typing in Iron Teeth Indian Women and reading the amazing interview of her by Thomas B. Marquis.

A good glass of Chardonnay to Louise Vance, Carol Dannen and Colleen Hartman and all who had great ideas and who can join me at Table 12 anytime. I'll hand some cold lemonade to Jim Campbell for the wonderful names.

To my sweetheart, Marv, and my kids. Thank you for loving me. I love you.

Be sure to visit Table 12 at www.theboobgirls.com.

All the girls blog and sometimes Wes and Wiley get a word or two in as well. I would love to be in touch with you. www.welcometotheboobgirls.blogspot.com

Contact Joy to speak to your group (or to just say hello) through the website: www.theboobgirls.com or by email at joy.johnson@msn.com.